# Kernowland

## The Crystal Pool

Titles available in the Kernowland series:

*Kernowland 1 The Crystal Pool*
*Kernowland 2 Darkness Day*
*Kernowland 3 Invasion of Evil*
*Kernowland 4 Pigleg's Revenge*
*Kernowland 5 Slavechildren*
*Kernowland 6 Colosseum of Dread*

Titles available in the 13 Things series:

*The Emperor's Rhinoceros*

To Sara

# Kernowland
## The Crystal Pool

Jack Trelawny

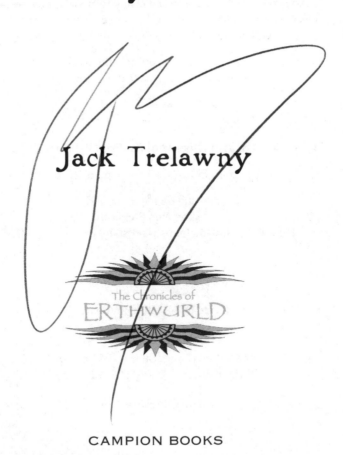

The Chronicles of
ERTHWURLD

CAMPION BOOKS

A catalogue record for this book
is available from the British Library

ISBN 978-1-906815-01-1


Campion Books is an Imprint of Campion Publishing Limited

Illustrations by Louise Hackman-Hexter

Printed and bound in the UK by
Short Run Press Ltd,
Bittern Rd, Sowton Industrial Estate, Exeter, EX2 7LW


First printed in paperback 2013

First published in the UK in hardback 2005 by

**CAMPION BOOKS**
2 Lea Valley House, Stoney Bridge Drive,
Waltham Abbey, Essex, UK   EN9 3LY


www.jacktrelawny.com

For Tizzie and Louis

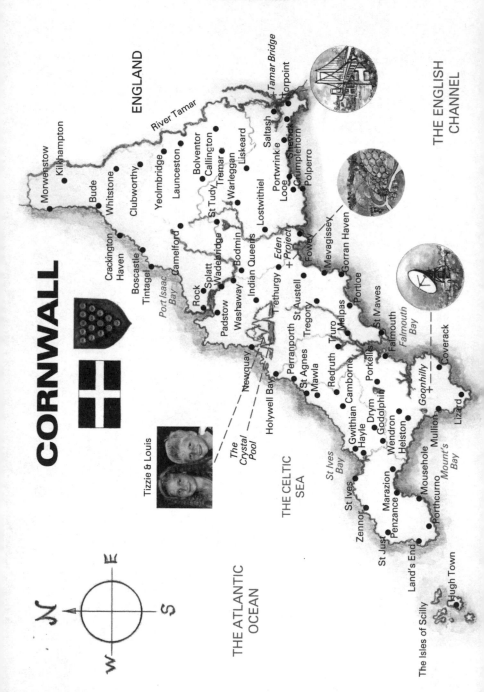

Kernowland

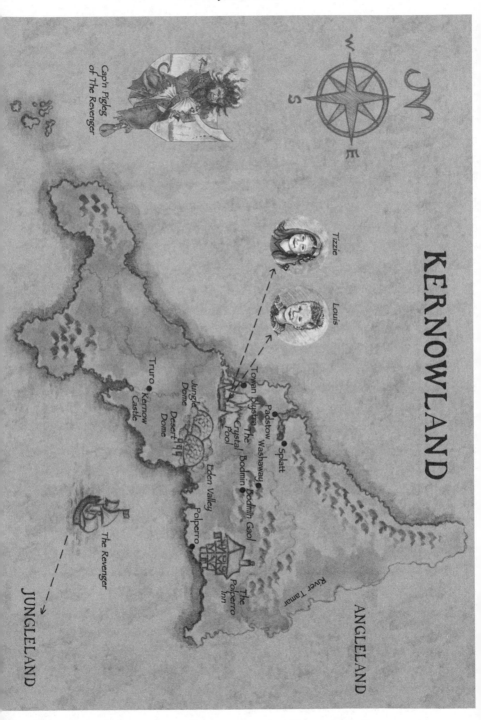

# AUTHOR'S NOTES

Apart from Tizzie & Louis,
the characters and events in this book
are entirely fictitious.

In the *Erthwurld* books,
'Erth' means 'Earth',
and 'Wurld' means 'World'.
*Evile* is pronounced *ee-vile* to rhyme with mile.
*Skotos* is pronounced *skoh-toss* – it means 'darkness' in Greek.
*Photos* is pronounced *foh-toss* – it means 'of light' in Greek.
*Graph* means 'draw' in Greek, so a *photograph* is...
'a picture drawn with light'.

### *Websites*
There is lots of other information
as well as clickable zooming maps
on the Kernowland and Erthwurld websites

**www.kernowland.com**
**www.erthwurld.com**

# Characters

Lots of characters in the *Kernowland in Erthwurld* series have either first or second names that I have taken from the names of places in Cornwall.

On my school visits, I speak to children whose families come from countries all around the world, so the characters in this series are inspired by the people of many countries and all the continents.

## Here are two challenges for you:

### Challenge 1

First, look at the Cornwall map at the front of this book and try to remember as many names of cities, towns, and villages as you can. Then - when you are reading the story - see if you can spot the characters who have names that are on the Cornwall map.

### Challenge 2

As you are reading the story, see if you can spot at least five countries that have inspired me to create characters.

There are large colour versions of all the *Kernowland in Erthwurld* maps on our website:

# www.jacktrelawny.com

# Kernowland

## An adventure in Erthwurld

See the sections at the back for illustrations of scenes and characters from the *Kernowland in Erthwurld* series...

as well as information about Jack Trelawny's new series, *13 Things*... and his **FREE school author visits**...

## The Crystal Pool

# ONE

## Are We Nearly There Yet?

'Are we nearly there yet?' moaned Louis, for the twelfth time.

'Stop asking that,' scolded Tizzie, 'you *are* nearly eight, you know.'

'Not long now,' said Mr Bennett, smiling patiently.

Anastasia Bennett was called 'Tizzie' for short. She was nearly eleven years old; and her brother, Louis – who always had to tell people how to say his name, *'Lew-eee'* not *'Lew-iss'*, when he first met them – was seven-and-three-quarters.

The Bennett family were going on holiday in their car.

As they passed over the long bridge that spanned the River Tamar, there was a sign which had two words on it – *Cornwall* and *Kernow*.

'Kernow is the old Cornish language name for Cornwall,' explained Mr Bennett. 'We'll soon be in the town of Newquay, which was once called Towan Blystra.'

My Dad knows everything, thought Tizzie.

'Yes, and my friend Todd said there are real gnomes in Cornwall,' enthused Louis. 'They live in people's gardens and come alive at night. And there are trolls and sea monsters and little people called "piskies" that only children can see.'

My brother doesn't know anything, thought Tizzie.

'Be a good girl and amuse your brother for a while,' said Mum, handing her daughter a booklet. 'Here, show him all about *The Eden Project*. We're going there tomorrow morning.'

11

'Look at these two huge white domes, Louis,' said Tizzie, pointing at the front page of the booklet.

Louis looked, as Tizzie continued.

'They're so big that one has a jungle in it, and the other has a desert.'

Louis was puzzled.

'How can they have a jungle and a desert in them?'

'Because the scientists make it so that the climate is like a real jungle in one dome, and like a desert in the other,' explained Tizzie.

'What's a climate?' queried Louis.

'It's the weather and temperature in a particular place,' answered Tizzie. 'It's warm and wet in the jungle, and hot and dry in the desert.'

Louis gave her one of his confused looks.

'But where do they get the plants?'

'They collect them from all over the world and put them in the big white domes to live,' said Tizzie. 'They've even brought back carnivorous plants from some places.'

'What's carnivorous?' asked Louis, screwing up his face because he'd never heard that word before.

'It means "meat-eating",' answered his sister. 'If you get too close, they'll eat you, Louis; they like eating little boys.'

'No way,' shrugged Louis, pretending not to be bothered.

'Stop frightening your brother, Tizzie,' cautioned Mum. 'You know he has nightmares.'

Tizzie went quiet, reading all about *The Eden Project* for the rest of the journey.

Louis was quiet too. He was thinking about carnivorous plants, and wondering whether they really could eat people.

# TWO

## Echo Cave

An hour after crossing the Tamar Bridge, the Bennetts arrived at the hotel and parked the car.

When they were unpacked, Mrs Bennett asked them what they wanted to do first.

'Beach,' said Tizzie.

'Beach,' said Louis.

'Beach,' said Dad.

'Beach it is then,' said Mum, with a big smile.

Mrs Bennett made sure they had everything ready: the surfboard, the blow-up shark, Louis' float, the big towels, and the picnic basket.

Then she picked up her little red beach bag, and led the way to the front of the hotel.

On the short walk to the beach, Louis looked at the seagulls, Tizzie listened to the roar of the sea, Dad smelt the fish and chips, and Mum admired the wonderful view over the bay.

When they arrived at the beach, Louis and Tizzie changed into their swimming costumes and asked if they could go exploring before they went in the water.

'All right, but make sure you can see us all the time,' warned Dad.

'Race,' shouted Tizzie, and set off running towards a big cave with Louis chasing after her. Tizzie was a very good big sister and she slowed down a little so that she and Louis both got to the mouth of the cave at exactly the same time.

For some reason though, Tizzie was hesitant to go any further; she had a strange feeling that something was wrong.

As usual, Louis just went straight in, with neither thought nor feeling to hinder his progress.

'Come out of there, Louis,' pleaded Tizzie. 'Dad said we must be able to see them all the time.'

'I *can* see Mum and Dad from in here,' reported Louis, from atop a pointed rock towards the back of the cave, his words echoing around the walls to his obvious delight. 'Come in and stand on this rock and you'll see I'm telling the truth. Or are you scared?'

Despite her own reservations, and although she thought Dad might be cross, Tizzie made herself go into the cave. She was determined not to be called a 'scaredycat' by her little brother. He'd definitely go on about it for the whole holiday if she didn't go in.

On braving the cave, Tizzie saw Louis' pointed rock, which was covered in seaweed and surrounded by a little pool. Drips of water plopped into the pool from the roof of the cave, making ripples as they splashed.

She put her toe in the water and immediately took it out.

'I can't do that, it's freezing,' she complained.

'Close your eyes and it doesn't feel as cold,' advised Louis. 'That's what I did.'

Tizzie didn't think that closing her eyes would stop the pool being cold, but tried it anyway. She summoned all her courage and stepped into the water. It was just as cold with her eyes closed.

She waded five shivering steps to the rock, and Louis stretched out his hand to help her climb up it.

Tizzie and Louis stood on the big rock surrounded by the icy cold pool.

Pop! Pop!

The seaweed covering the rock popped every time they moved their feet.

'Hellllowwwww,' shouted Louis.

'Hellllowwwww,' replied the cave.

'I'm going to call it "Echo Cave",' declared Louis.

'Okay,' agreed his sister, 'that's a good name.'

Inside the cave, it was very dark. They both looked out towards the bright and sunny beach.

'It's like looking out of a tunnel,' said Louis.

'Yes,' said Tizzie, 'and the good thing is, we can still see Mum and Dad.'

Suddenly, they heard a rustling sound from the back of the cave.

Someone, or some *thing*, was in there with them.

# THREE

## Gwithian Sand

'Who's there?' whispered Tizzie.

'It could be a cave monster!' exclaimed Louis, as if half-hoping it would be.

There was another rustling sound at the back of the cave.

Tizzie wanted to run away and tell Mum and Dad, but Louis was already clambering over rocks towards the sound.

'Come back, Louis,' she pleaded, but Louis just kept on going, and Tizzie knew she had to follow. Even though they were always arguing, Tizzie loved Louis really and she couldn't just leave him there, especially if he might be in danger.

So she followed her little brother into the darkness and took his hand for comfort as they went further and further and further into the cave.

It got darker and darker, and colder and colder, as they stumbled over wet slippery rocks.

Soon the cave became more like a tunnel, with a flat, sandy floor.

Whoooooshh.

They heard the faint whistling of wind up ahead.

The further in they went, the more the wind gusted down the tunnel towards them, blowing Tizzie's long fair hair off her ears.

'Please let's go back,' pleaded Tizzie, 'I'm really scared.'

'Oh why,' protested Louis, his teeth chattering as the wind began to scream and howl and make his swimming shorts flap against his legs. 'Can't we go on just a little bit further?'

Boom!

Flash!

Before they could go on or back another step, there was a loud noise, accompanied by a very bright spark of light. They were dazzled for a few moments as a huge puff of yellow smoke began to engulf them.

Tizzie and Louis huddled together and shivered in the smoke, gripping each other even more tightly as a voice from the darkness startled them.

'So sorry, didn't mean to frighten you. Just lighting my glow-crystal.'

With that, a little ball of golden light began to glow in the smoke. It was a couple of feet off the ground and shone brightly from a tiny yellow stone, held in the upturned palm of a very small hand.

The light became even brighter, allowing them to see who was speaking. It was a diminutive man, not much taller than Louis, with bow-legs, and extra large ears which stuck out at the sides of his long, grey, bushy beard. He wore a monocle in his right eye, and squinted at them through it.

'Who are you?' asked Tizzie.

'What are you?' asked Louis, 'a pisky?'

'I most certainly am not,' replied the little man, apparently offended, 'troublesome little things, piskies. Let me introduce myself. I am Gwithian Sand, the King's Chief Surveyor and Mapmaker.' As the man spoke, he gave a little bow.

'But we have a Queen, not a King, at the moment,' quizzed Tizzie suspiciously.

'Yes, that's right, the Queen of Cornwall,' spouted Louis, as if he knew something important.

My brother really *doesn't* know anything at all, thought Tizzie.

'Aha, but I am not from *Cornwall*,' explained Mr Sand. 'I am from the land of *Kernow*.'

'But they're the same place,' complained Tizzie, remembering what her Dad had said in the car at the big bridge.

'Not right, well... not quite,' informed the little man, whose big ears and stubby nose and bushy eyebrows all twitched together as he spoke. 'Kernowland is like Cornwall in some ways, but it is altogether a very different place.'

'What's it like?' asked Louis, enthusiastically. He believed the little man without question; because he wanted to believe.

'Kernowland is a place of wonder and magic,' enthused Mr Sand with a big, friendly smile.

'And just *where* is this Kernowland supposed to *be*?' queried Tizzie, in her most important sounding voice, whilst at the same time trying not to sound rude. 'And if you live *there*, what are you doing *here*?'

'I'm... I'm just exploring the caves,' stuttered Mr Sand, as if a bit flummoxed and flustered by Tizzie's tone.

'Anyway, have to be on my way now, must get back to Kernowland. Take this glow-crystal and you will be able to find your way back to the beach.

'Bye-bye, children.'

Gwithian Sand turned about and hurried off down the tunnel, waddling as fast as his little legs could carry him.

When he neared a bend, he glanced back over his shoulder, as if to make sure they weren't following him, then rounded the corner and disappeared out of sight.

# FOUR

## The Glistening Cavern

'Better get back to the beach, Louis,' suggested Tizzie, sensibly.

'I want to go to Kernowland,' insisted Louis.

Without giving his sister a chance to reply, he set off in the direction in which Mr Sand had gone.

'But you've got no light,' shouted Tizzie after him. 'You won't be able to see in the dark.'

When she caught up with her brother, Tizzie scolded him like she thought big sisters are supposed to.

'Come back now, Louis. We don't know what's down the tunnel. It could be dangerous.'

'But I just want to see where Kernowland is,' sighed Louis. 'Please, Tizzie, please.'

Tizzie found it hard to say no to her brother when he said 'please', but still tried one last time to reason with him.

'There is no Kernowland, Louis. That man made up a story because you're a little boy.'

'Why did he have a crystal that glows in the dark then?' countered Louis. Tizzie had to admit that it was quite a good question, and she hadn't actually thought about it herself.

'Oh, all right. We can go on for a few more minutes. But you'll see, there'll be nothing down that tunnel except more rocks. And don't blame me if you stub your toe on something. Here, you take the light.'

Louis held the glow-crystal in his right hand and lit the way. Tizzie held her brother's left hand again, this time squeezing it just a little as they continued on down the tunnel.

After what seemed like ages, they came upon a big open cavern. Tizzie looked around in awe; she had never seen anything like it. The walls were set with glistening stones, in all the colours of the rainbow.

Louis looked up.

'It's so high; I can only just see the top.'

A familiar voice echoed through the cavern, and attracted their attention to a large recess in the wall.

'Oh dear me.'

'Look, it's Mr Sand!' exclaimed Tizzie, pointing her finger.

The Bennett children stared, transfixed, hardly able to believe their own eyes.

Mr Sand was in a pool of steaming blue liquid. Through a misty blue haze, they saw that only his head was above the surface of the pool.

He was looking in their direction with an expression of great worry on his face, as if concerned that they should see him doing what he was doing.

'Do you need help, Mr Sand?' shouted Tizzie.

'Oh dear, oh dear. No, no, nooo. Go away children, go away. It's very important that you don't…'

With that, Mr Sand's mouth sank into the pool before he could finish his sentence.

# FIVE

## The Crystal Pool

Louis ran towards Mr Sand but, by the time he got there, the weird little man's head was completely submerged.

Strangely, what had been a pool of blue liquid only moments earlier, was now a solid slab of blue rock, which sparkled and twinkled even brighter than the cavern walls.

Before Tizzie could stop him, Louis was standing on the slab, stamping his foot up and down on the solid stone.

'How did he disappear into it, Tizzie? It's all hard.'

'I don't know, Louis. Now just get down off there.'

'You can't make me.'

'Oh yes I can, young man,' admonished Tizzie, in a voice she had heard her mother use so often.

She stepped on to the blue slab to try to move Louis off it.

'Don't be silly, Louis. Let's go back to the beach. I really have had enough of this now.'

'But I want to go to KERNOWLAND,' shouted her little brother.

Sssssssssssss.

At that very instant, the hard blue rock beneath their feet began to hiss. Tizzie screamed and tried to step off it, but the rock was now sticky like glue, and her feet were stuck to it.

The rock got softer and softer until it was like runny jelly at the top but still quite firm under their feet. It frothed and bubbled as blue steam rose all around them.

The children started to sink.

Tizzie and Louis squirmed and wriggled, but they just couldn't stop themselves sinking and sinking. For the first time that afternoon, Tizzie thought Louis looked *really* scared.

As they sank deeper and deeper into the steaming blue pool, Louis whispered something which Tizzie could only just hear.

'I think I said the password.'

They were now up to their waists in the bubbling liquid. Tizzie tried to think for both of them.

'Bend your knees and jump up as high as you can and try to grab on to the side and pull yourself up, Louis,' she instructed.

She tried. Louis tried. Their feet were still stuck to the hard part of the rock.

'I can't do it, I just can't,' shouted Louis, with a look of panic on his face.

'Whatever you do, Louis, hold your breath for as long as you can… And close your eyes… And pinch your nose like this.'

Copying Tizzie, Louis put his fingers over his nose and squeezed. His chin started to sink into the rock before Tizzie's because he was shorter than her.

'I'm scared,' he whimpered.

'Just hold your breath,' said Tizzie. 'Hold your breath.' She wasn't quite sure why, but she also said: 'You're the best brother in the world, Louis.'

Tizzie watched in horror as her brother's head went under the surface of the steaming, frothing, bubbling blue liquid. She held her breath as it began to cover her chin.

A little tear welled in her eye and she began to cry.

'I don't want us to die,' she sobbed quietly.

# SIX

## Still Alive

Then, for no apparent reason, the hard part of the rock under their feet began to rise up again.

Tizzie emerged from the bubbling, fizzing blue pool before Louis. First the top of her head, then her brow. When her eyes rose above the surface, she opened them and looked around. Just a few more seconds to hold her breath and she would still be alive.

'Ahhh,' she gasped, as her mouth was once more able to breathe air.

She hoped and hoped that Louis would be all right. It seemed like ages that they had been under the surface.

Then Louis' head emerged from the pool, followed by the rest of him.

The pool began to solidify under their feet and soon, after a lot more hissing, they were standing on a firm slab of twinkling, sparkling blue rock again.

'Ohhh Louis, you're all right,' sighed Tizzie, as she put her arms around her brother in a gesture of relief.

'Yeah,' said Louis, nonchalantly, trying to wriggle away from his sister's hug.

'I didn't know you could hold your breath for so long, Louis. You were in there longer than me. Well done.'

'I can't,' admitted Louis. 'When I couldn't hold my breath any more, I just started breathing. It was easy.'

Tizzie gave Louis one of her 'don't be so silly' looks, so he changed the subject.

'Where are we? Do you think this is Kernowland?'

'Sshhh!' said Tizzie, putting her hand over his mouth. 'That was the word that made us sink into the rock before.'

They both looked at each other expectantly, and got ready to sink again. This time though, the word didn't have any effect. The rock didn't hiss or steam or get sticky or soft; it just stayed as it was, hard and cold.

Tizzie sighed with relief. From the look on his face, she could see that Louis was slightly disappointed.

'I'd still like to go to KERNOWLAND,' he shouted defiantly, as if having one last go at getting there.

'Look, we're in exactly the same place as before,' reasoned Tizzie. 'The cavern is exactly the same and you've still got the glow-crystal.'

'What should we do now?'

'We'll use the glow-crystal to get back through the dark tunnel to Echo Cave. Then we can throw the crystal away and go and see Mum and Dad.'

'They're going to be cross that we've been so long.'

'Yes, so you'd better not tell them about Mr Sand and the glow-crystal and the sinking rock. Agreed?'

'Agreed,' nodded Louis. He certainly didn't want to get into any more trouble than they were in already.

'Right, so give me the crystal.'

As Louis handed over the glowing yellow crystal, Tizzie noticed that its light had got much dimmer. 'It looks like it might go out soon. We'll have to hurry.'

They set off down the tunnel back towards the beach. There had been no wind in the high cavern but, for some reason, the long tunnel was very windy, just as it had been before. The howling wind pushed them along from behind.

They reached Echo Cave just as the light from the glow-crystal finally went out.

The sunlight streamed in through the cave entrance. Tizzie threw the little crystal over her head towards the back of the cave, where it plopped into the icy cold pool.

'Right, let's go and see Mum and Dad,' she sighed, very relieved to have got back to where they started from.

But, as they looked out from the cave along the beach, there was no one to be seen.

The buckets and spades had gone.

The people and towels had gone.

The ice cream van had gone.

Mum and Dad... had gone.

# SEVEN

## Bumps on the Beach

Outside Echo Cave, thunder roared overhead as it began to pour with rain. Heavy droplets pelted down on the rocks.

A waterfall soon covered the cave entrance like a big wet curtain. Tizzie and Louis glimpsed the deserted beach through the torrent of water.

'Mum and Dad and everyone else must have gone because they thought it was going to rain,' said Tizzie, trying to make Louis feel better.

'But why did they leave us here?' worried Louis.

'Because you're with me and they know I'm old enough to be sensible,' reassured Tizzie, not quite sure that she was entirely right. 'When the rain stops, we can go across the beach and up the cliff steps to the town. The hotel isn't far.'

'Okay,' agreed Louis, 'I just want to see Mum and Dad now.'

While they waited, Louis started asking 'who', 'what', and 'why' questions. He was always doing that when he was curious or bothered about something, and Tizzie usually dismissed him as much as possible, as if she wasn't really interested in his childish questions.

But, secretly, with all that had happened, she was now a little bit more interested in finding out the answers herself.

'Who do you think Mr Sand is, Tizzie?'

'He's probably a Cornish person who likes going in caves and scaring little children like you.'

'But why was he so short? And why did he have such

funny clothes? And that funny hat? I think he could be a gnome.'

'Lots of Cornish people are short. And gnomes aren't real.'

'What about the glow-crystal? Crystals don't do that on their own.'

'It was probably a toy, something from a joke shop. It might have had a tiny battery somewhere inside it.'

'I'm going to find it again,' decided Louis, before making his way towards the back of the cave. It was darker there, and he couldn't see too well. He started paddling around in the icy pool, trying to find the little yellow crystal with his feet as he asked more questions.

'What sort of rock do you think that round blue rock is?'

'I don't know. But there are lots of things we don't know. Grown-ups probably know all about them, but we can't ask anyone because you promised not to, didn't you, Louis? We'll look it up on the internet when we get home.'

'But rocks don't go soft, and you can't slide into them, and you can't breathe inside them, and...'

'We don't know that for certain, Louis. Let's just wait and see. Come on, the rain has stopped.'

They stepped out of the cave into bright sunshine.

'Look,' said Louis, pointing up to the sky.

There, flying low and heading for the cliffs, was a huge black bird with a red beak and red feet. They could hear the sound of its wings flapping.

'It's as big as a horse!' exclaimed Tizzie.

The sun glared in their eyes, making it difficult to see clearly.

Louis wasn't sure, but he thought there was a man riding in a saddle on the bird's back.

'We *have* come to another place, Tizzie,' he said in

amazement. 'It must be Kernowland.'

'I don't want to talk about it anymore,' replied Tizzie, not wanting to believe the evidence of her own eyes.

'What's that?' screeched Louis, suddenly grabbing his sister's arm and making her jump.

Tizzie looked and saw her brother was pointing at the ground, his finger trembling.

All around them the grains of sand were moving.

The beach began to rise up in little bumps.

The little bumps turned into bigger bumps.

As the bumps grew and grew, a huge pink-red claw rose out of one of them and snapped open and shut. Two large, cold, black eyes followed it. Then a pair of pincers emerged in front of a big mouth.

All around them, claws and black eyes and pincers and big mouths were rising out of the sand.

Suddenly, the sand right under their feet started to shift and rise up.

'Run, Louis,' shouted Tizzie in terror.

'They're giant crabs!'

# EIGHT

## The Knotted Rope

Tizzie jumped off the rising sand and ran towards the cliff where the steps had been. Louis followed as fast as he could. Behind them the giant crabs were now completely out of the sand and chasing them up the beach. The crabs moved sideways, snapping their claws and making a squeaking noise with their pincers as they moved them in and out.

Louis glanced behind him. The crabs were opening and shutting their red mouths, which dripped with a gooey liquid, as if they were hungry.

'Ahhh!' Louis cried out.

Tizzie looked behind her to see Louis sitting on the sand clutching his foot. It was bleeding. He had tripped and fallen about halfway to the cliff.

A tear welled in his eye as the blood trickled between his fingers.

'Help me, Tizzie,' he shouted, 'I've cut my foot on a shell.'

Louis tried to get up. In his haste, he slipped on the sand again and fell back down.

Tizzie ran to help him. She now saw that lots of blood was oozing from the cut. Tizzie put Louis' arm around her shoulders and helped him get to his feet. He began to hop up the beach towards the cliff, with Tizzie helping him as much as she could. But the two of them were going much slower now.

The crabs were gaining ground and catching up with every second. Tizzie heard the snapping of the claws and the squeaking of the pincers getting nearer.

'Faster, Louis; we must go faster.'

Finally, they got to the part of the cliff where the steps had been.

'Where are the steps?' whimpered Louis.

'They've gone; we'll have to climb up instead,' urged Tizzie, as she began to scramble up the cliff. 'Come on, Louis.'

Louis reached out his hands and put his good foot on the rock. Then he took hold and pulled himself up and put his bad foot down on it.

'Ouch!'

Tizzie heard Louis cry out as she continued up the cliff.

'Quicker, Louis, we must climb higher to get out of reach of the crabs.'

'I'm trying, but my foot hurts.'

'Here, take my hand,' offered Tizzie, stretching out her arm.

As her brother took her left hand, Tizzie held on tightly with her right and pulled as hard as she could.

It was lucky she did because a giant crab was just about to snap its claws onto Louis' leg.

Clunk! The claws came together with a crunch.

When this crab missed clamping on to Louis' leg, it seemed to give up and just lay down at the bottom of the cliff face.

Tizzie was relieved to see that the crabs weren't trying to get them anymore.

But then she saw that a second giant crab climbed onto the back of the first. And a third climbed onto the back of the second.

Tizzie couldn't believe it. The giant crabs seemed to be building a piggy-back tower in order to reach them.

'As long as we can climb up and get to the top, we'll be okay,' she assured Louis, although her whole body was shaking with fear as she continued to climb in panic. Glancing down, she saw that the crabs were only inches away from Louis' feet.

'Faster, Louis; climb faster.'

'I'm trying!'

Just then, a thick rope with lots of knots along it, flopped down beside them.

Someone shouted from the top of the cliff.

'Hold on, children, we'll soon have you out of there.'

'Grab the rope, Louis,' screamed Tizzie, as she grabbed hold of it herself, without really thinking.

'I've got it,' shouted Louis from below.

'Pull us up, please, please,' screamed Tizzie.

The rope started to move upwards, with the two children hanging on tightly.

They were halfway to the top of the cliff before Tizzie thought of something which she whispered down to Louis as quietly as she could.

'We don't know who it is up there.'

# NINE

## Melanchol Drym and Spikey

As they neared the top of the cliff, Tizzie became more and more worried about who was pulling on the other end of the rope.

When they reached the top, the last bit was grassy and her head was suddenly being dragged through the grass, forcing her to close her eyes.

When she opened them, she saw who had been pulling on the rope. It was a man with grey skin and a horrible smirk on his face.

'Run, Louis. RUN!'

But the tall, skinny man had long, gangly arms and he grabbed them both by the ears with his grey, bony fingers as they tried to get away; Louis by his left ear and Tizzie by her right. He lifted his hands up so that they both had to stand on tiptoe to stop it hurting so much.

'Ah, what have we here, Dribble?' he sneered to his dog. 'Kids with golden hair. I've never seen the like of these two before.

'They'll likely fetch a good price at the slave market.

'Pigleg will pay handsomely for them, I'm sure. Oh yes he will.'

'Grrrrr,' growled Dribble, as if he disapproved of what was happening. The man snarled and kicked the poor little dog with his pointed shoes. The dog yelped and cowered submissively. Tizzie hoped the man would not hurt the little dog again.

'Yessss, very good price,' said the man, menacingly,

bringing his long pointed nose right in front of Tizzie's face. He stared at her with his cold, dark, bloodshot eyes, and she was so scared she began to sob.

Louis saw that the man was frightening his big sister. He tried to be brave.

'Let her go,' he shouted in his deepest voice, as he tried to kick the man in the shins and punch him in the tummy; but the man just pulled on Louis' ear a little harder, and he had to stop kicking and punching because it really hurt.

'Let us go, please,' begged Tizzie. 'We haven't done anything wrong.'

'All children have done something wrong; oh yes they have,' growled the man as he dragged them screaming towards a track that was a few yards from the cliff edge.

Tizzie saw that, one way, the track led down to a little town of round houses with thatched, cone-shaped roofs. A sign pointing in that direction showed that it was: *Towan Blystra*.

The other way, the track went around a hill which rose above the cliff, so she couldn't see what was on the other side.

Tizzie looked at the man's rickety wooden cart. Harnessed at the front was a scruffy-looking brown horse. The back of the cart was filled with all sorts of rubbish. The man pointed to a pile of rotten old rags.

'Get in there and put those clothes on,' he said. 'Out here in this weather in your underwear. Whatever next? Don't want you to get sick, do we? Oh no we don't. Want you in prime condition for the market, oh yes we do.'

Tizzie and Louis didn't move.

'You'll do as I say or you'll feel the wrath of Spikey; oh yes you will,' growled the man.

They both looked at the pointed stick that the man was

33

wielding. Tizzie nodded to Louis that she thought it best to do as they were told.

The man grinned another horrible grin.

'That's better. They don't like the look of you, do they Spikey? Oh no they don't.'

When Tizzie and Louis had chosen and put on their smelly old rags, the man clicked thick, iron rings around their ankles and turned a big key in the locks. They were now securely shackled to the cart.

The stench of the rubbish was horrible.

The man tore off some strips from other old clothes in the pile. He rolled the strips up, climbed on the cart, and tied Louis' hands together. Then he put the middle of one strip in Louis' mouth and tied the two ends behind his head.

Louis' foot was still bleeding. He was trembling, and Tizzie felt very protective towards her little brother.

'Please don't put that on him, sir, we promise to be quiet,' she pleaded.

'Ha, kids always make promises they don't keep,' he sneered. 'Do you think I was born yesterday, little lady? Well I wasn't, oh no I wasn't.'

As he tied Tizzie's hands together and put a gag in her mouth, she noticed for the first time that the man smelt worse than the rubbish in his cart.

The man got out of the cart and wagged his long, thin, dirty-nailed finger at them threateningly.

'No one will know you're in there unless you make a sound. So, if you make so much as a mouse-squeak, I promise you, you'll get to know Spikey a whole lot better… and Melanchol Drym always keeps his promises. Oh… Yes… He… Does.'

At that very moment, thunder roared overhead, and lightning flashed as the storm started anew.

Tizzie's eyes met Louis'. She tried to reassure him with her gaze, but she could see he was petrified.

Then a big canvas cover was pulled over the back of the cart, and they were in darkness.

# TEN

# The Polperro Inn

They travelled on and on through the night. The rain pelted down on the cover, and one of the big wheels of the cart squeaked on every turn so they couldn't even get a minute of sleep.

Tizzie could feel the changes in direction as the cart went around bends and rattled up and down hills. Occasionally it bumped and banged over cobbles, which made her think they might be going through towns as well as countryside.

When the rain stopped, she hoped she might hear someone friendly. But all was quiet. There was not so much as a whisper from outside, and Tizzie started to think they were never going to escape.

She didn't want to be a slave. Questions raced through her mind. Where were they being taken? Who was Pigleg?

It seemed like the smelly, rickety, old wooden cart had been going on forever before they rattled over hundreds of cobbles as they bumped and banged down a steep hill.

Tizzie heard the sound of lots of people who seemed to be having some sort of party. The noise got louder and louder as they approached the bottom of the hill.

The cart stopped, and Tizzie could now hear that the people were shouting and singing at the top of their voices.

Inside the cart, under the cover, it had been pitch black all the way but Tizzie could now just see through a tiny hole that there were flickering lights outside.

She heard Melanchol Drym jump from the front of the cart. His heels clicked on the cobbles as he strode slowly round to the back.

The nasty man lifted the cover. A flaming torch in his hand lit up his greasy black hair and horrible grey face. Tizzie had to squint because the light was so bright.

'Right, let's get you out of there,' he said coldly, as he threw back the cover, climbed on the cart and turned the key in the shackles around their ankles.

'We'll get 'em sold off quickly tonight, Dribble, oh yes we will. Lots of crews in port, oh yes there are. Ten crowns apiece we'll get for golden-haired children, oh yes we will.'

Leaving their hands tied, and gags on, Drym pulled them by their ears again to make them stand up.

Tizzie winced as she was forced to her feet. She could now see where the lights were coming from.

There was a sign over the door: *The Polperro Inn.*

Drym forced them down off the cart, and dragged them across the cobbles, pulling roughly on their ears all the while.

'Heel, Dribble,' growled the grey man, pointing to the back of his dirty black shoe. The little sausage dog did as he was told.

They went under an arch and round to the back of the inn. Here Drym discarded his torch and gave three strange knocks as if it were some sort of signal.

A fat, rosy-cheeked woman came to the door carrying a lantern. She wore a low-cut blouse, and a full-length skirt which dropped down to her ankles.

Tizzie thought she looked like someone from three hundred years ago, or even more.

'Why, Mr Drym, what brings you all the way to Polperro at such a late hour?' questioned the woman, in such a manner that Tizzie thought she already knew the answer.

'Good evening, Mrs Maggitt,' said Drym, as he tugged on Tizzie and Louis' ears so they came into the light of the lantern at the door.

'I'm seeking the opinion of a ship's captain, as to the value of two small animals I have for sale. Usual share for you and Mr Maggitt, of course.'

'Oh, well, you should have said sooner,' said Mrs Maggitt, grinning greedily, eyeing Tizzie and Louis as if she were hungry and just about to eat her dinner.

'You don't often see golden hair like that in Kernowland, Mr Drym. They look to me like Angles from east of the Tamar. What are you doing with them?'

'Washed up on the beach, oh yes they did,' said Drym, as he dragged Tizzie and Louis into the back room of the inn. 'I saved them from the climbing crabs, and now they're going to repay me, oh yes they are.'

Tizzie didn't like the look of Mrs Maggitt any more than she liked Drym, but she was desperate and tried to ask for help.

'Mmm... mmm.'

But the sound came out all muffled by the gag in her mouth.

Melanchol Drym glared down at her and nodded to the pointed stick that was stuck in his belt.

'Remember I have Spikey with me at all times, oh yes I have.'

Tizzie wanted to hold Louis' hand to give him some comfort. He seemed to have given up now, and was just looking at the ground all the time.

She looked at the ground too, so as not to give their captors any reason to hurt them.

Mrs Maggitt led them through another dark room with her lantern. Then she opened another door and, suddenly, they were in the main room of the inn, which had a very low ceiling and exposed timber beams.

Tizzie choked a little and raised her head in the dimly lit, smoke-filled room.

All the noise and talking and singing stopped.

A fire crinkled and crackled in the corner.

Everyone was staring at them.

They looked like pirates.

# ELEVEN

## Slaves

What 'ave we 'ere, Mrs Maggitt?' asked a stout man wearing a big apron with blood stains all over it. Tizzie thought he looked like a butcher.

'Why, Mr Maggitt, we 'ave some small creatures for sale, property of Mr Melanchol Drym,' said his wife.

'Well, well. What a pleasant surprise on this dull evening. Bring 'em forward so we can all assess their value.'

Some of the people moved the tables to the side, leaving only one chair in the middle of the room. All the people now formed a circle around the chair. The noise got louder as the excitement grew.

Drym needed no further encouragement. He pulled Tizzie and Louis forward by their ears and removed Tizzie's gag and ties, throwing them to Dribble who caught them in his mouth.

Drym then pushed Tizzie into the centre.

'Ladies first,' he sneered. 'Stand on that chair.'

Tizzie did as she was told. She looked at the floor, quivering from her head to her toes.

A pirate with a bald head rose to his feet and paced slowly over to the chair. He was a very big man, with rippling muscles bulging underneath his shirt. He was a foot taller than Tizzie, even though she was standing on the chair.

His left arm stopped at the elbow and there was a piece of wood that looked like a truncheon attached to the stump.

'Ah, Mr Cudgel, delighted to see you again,' grovelled

Drym, rubbing his grey hands together and stooping a little. 'I trust Captain Pigleg is well. Please inspect the goods at your leisure.'

Cudgel sneered down at Drym as if he was something nasty and smelly stuck to his shoe.

He pulled Tizzie's chin up roughly with a thick finger on his right hand. Tizzie noticed that his little finger was missing, but all the other fingers had silver rings on them.

Then Mr Cudgel put his face so close to hers that she could smell his bad breath. He was chewing something brown that smelled a bit like cigarettes.

He pulled her mouth open.

'Fine set of pearls,' he mumbled, as if surprised at how nice and clean and white Tizzie's teeth were. 'Put out your tongue, slave.'

Tizzie put out her tongue.

Then Mr Cudgel squeezed her arms.

'Not much muscle. No use in the Caveland mines, this one, wouldn't last a week.'

'Oh, but Mr Cudgel, look at that golden hair and pretty face,' snivelled Drym in a worried voice. 'She'd make a wonderful wife for the Sultan of Sandland.'

'Hmmm, that's true enough,' mused Mr Cudgel. 'The Cap'n will be pleased with the purchase, I'm sure.'

'I don't want to be married,' protested Tizzie, as she began to cry. 'I just want to go home.'

Everyone in the room roared with laughter.

'It speaks back,' bellowed Mr Cudgel above the noise. 'We'll have to put a stop to that before we can sell 'er on.'

Melanchol Drym glared at Tizzie.

'Speak when you're spoken to, slave,' he spat, drawing Spikey from his belt and resting its rusty iron point on the floor.

41

Tizzie knew this wasn't a game. She looked at the floor again.

Four more men and one woman came up to inspect her. They patted and prodded and pinched her. They looked in her eyes, pulled her ears, and squeezed her nose.

Drym glared all the while.

Tizzie kept quiet.

Then Mr Maggitt sat down at a table, picked up a pewter mug and banged it three times. All fell silent.

'Right then, ladies and gentlemen. As you can see we have here what appears to be a fine female specimen of Angle young. She'd not be much use in the mines, but she'd make a fine lady's maid in the castles of Mountainland. So let's start the bidding at five crowns, shall we?'

'Five crowns,' shouted someone from the back.

Tizzie could just see who had spoken. It was a big fat woman smoking a long thin pipe.

'Six,' said a man with one ear.

'Seven,' shouted a man with an eye patch.

The bidding went on. It got to ten crowns.

'Eleven,' bellowed Mr Cudgel.

There were no more bids.

Tizzie didn't want to be sold to Mr Cudgel. There was something very menacing about him.

She was in a daze. Everything had become too much for her.

'Sold to Mr Clubworthy Cudgel for eleven crowns,' she heard Mr Maggitt say, as he banged the mug down on the table very loudly.

Mr Cudgel dropped a bag of coins on the table, grabbed Tizzie's arm, tugged her off the chair, and dragged her towards the door.

Tizzie suddenly came to her senses.

She hadn't thought that she and Louis might be separated.

'What about my brother?' she pleaded, 'he's only little and he's frightened.'

'Best you forget about him,' warned Mr Cudgel. 'You'll not be seeing him again, I'll wager.'

As Cudgel reached the door, Tizzie heard Mr Maggitt shout out to the pirates.

'Right then, the next item for sale is a young male Angle. Looks like he'll grow into a strong slave for the mines of Caveland. Or perhaps an ice carrier in Snowland. Do I have a bid of five crowns?'

Louis glanced across at Tizzie.

She could see the fear in his eyes.

'Be brave, Louis,' she shouted, as she was hauled out roughly into the darkness of the night.

# TWELVE

## Big Red Grunter

Mr Cudgel pulled Tizzie along through the pouring rain. The sharp stones on the ground hurt her feet, and she kept stumbling.

'Come on, missy,' said the big man impatiently. 'You'll have to toughen up where you're going.'

Tizzie had at first thought they were heading towards the harbour, where there were a few boats moored. But Mr Cudgel had dragged her up some steep steps and they were now travelling along a cliff path in the opposite direction.

As they rounded a bend in the path, Tizzie saw a ship out to sea in the distance, its silhouette lit up by the moon. She didn't want to go on a ship. She wanted to go back to be with Louis.

'Please sir,' she asked, trying to be nice so that he would give her an answer, 'where are you taking me, and… and… who is Captain Pigleg?'

Suddenly, Mr Cudgel flew into a rage. He shook Tizzie by the shoulders and threw her to the ground.

As she lay petrified on the sandy path, thunder roared in the distance. Lightning flashed as Mr Cudgel pointed a thick finger at her and curled his lip.

'You'll speak when you're spoken to, slave,' he snarled. 'The Cap'n will teach you some manners with the lash, and no mistake.'

'I'm sorry, I'll be good,' promised Tizzie, trying to pacify the big, angry man. She didn't like the sound of the lash, which was a sort of whip as far as she knew.

'That's better,' growled Mr Cudgel, heaving Tizzie to her feet.

'Now, let me tell you about Cap'n Pigleg, so as you know the man who's to be your new master and you can show him some respect.

'He's the toughest, bravest, meanest pirate ever to sail the seas. You'll be wondering why they call him "Pigleg" won't you?

'Well the Cap'n had made port in Jungleland, see? Then he went a strollin' on a path near the jungle after visiting the local inn.

'Suddenly, out of the dark, shadowy trees, a wild boar moved on to the path; gruntin' and sniffin' and itchin' for battle.

'The Cap'n could see straight away it was the one the Junglelanders call Big Red Grunter, on account of his being thrice the size of any other boar in the jungle, with a hide redder 'n blood.

'Any other man would have been a dead man from sheer fear. But the Cap'n drew his cutlass and challenged the brute: "Come and taste my steel, Red Grunter, and I'll be eating yer flesh raw fer breakfast in the mornin'."

'Grunter put his head down and charged the Cap'n. There was a terrible fight.

'The beast has four long tusks, and teeth like razors. In one bite it chewed off the Cap'n's leg just below the knee, and the Cap'n fell to the ground.

'But the Cap'n was not going to die that night, not he. As the monster moved in for the kill, the Cap'n swung his cutlass and hacked away the pig's own front leg with one mighty swipe.

'Grunter let out a squeal to wake the very night itself, and hopped off back into the jungle.

'At daybreak, the search party found the Cap'n lying in a pool of blood. He had his cutlass in one hand, and Big Red's leg in the other.

'When the Cap'n awoke and saw he had no leg, he knew what he had to do. A leg for a leg, thought he, so the Cap'n cut off the flesh and made a pegleg from the blood-stained bone, with the beast's hoof still on the end of it.

'From that day on, he was known as "Cap'n Pigleg", and you can hear him coming by the click of his hoof on the ground every second step.

'And that's the legend that everybody in Kernowland and the whole of Erthwurld knows... except you, it seems.'

Tizzie's eyes opened as wide as they would go as she thought for a few moments about what she had just learned. She risked another question.

'Can I ask what happened to Grunter, sir?'

'Arr well, that's another story. The beast has become a mad thing. It terrorises the villages all over Jungleland. Hates humankind. Eats people whenever it can. And it 'specially likes taking the young children; the tender meat.

'But Grunter doesn't kill them quickly; no, he drags them into the jungle and eats them slowly... bit by bit by bit.

'That's why there is such a huge bounty on that great red boar. The Kingchief of Jungleland himself has offered a whole chest of treasure to whoever brings him its head.

'Cap'n Pigleg has made a vow to kill Big Red, whatever it takes. We're leaving on an expedition to Jungleland in the morning, taking a full cargo of bait... the juiciest child-meat we've been able to find around the wurld this past year.

'And that's where you come in, my little one... you're going to be boar bait.'

Tizzie went quiet, thinking deeply about everything Mr

Cudgel had told her. She could almost feel Big Red Grunter's teeth ripping and tearing at her flesh.

They carried on along the path through the rain until descending some steps hewn out of the rocks in a small cove. The waves pounded against the rocks and crashed on to the beach.

A little boat was on the sand. Mr Cudgel put Tizzie in the boat and pushed it into the water before jumping in himself. Slotting his truncheon arm into a special hole in one of the oars, and gripping the other with his good hand, he began to row towards the ship. He didn't say another word.

Tizzie decided to stay silent until spoken to.

The dark shadow of the ship loomed ever larger as they drew closer with each stroke of the oars. As they approached, Tizzie could just make out the letters written on the side of the hull: *The Revenger*.

A rope ladder dropped down over the side of the ship. Mr Cudgel waved his truncheon arm, motioning to Tizzie to climb up.

She did as she was told.

Looking up towards a light that shone over the side of the boat, she saw a man with a lantern peering down at her.

It was then that Tizzie heard the muffled cries of frightened children.

'Help us, please help us.'

# THIRTEEN

## Purgy

At the top of the ladder, the man with the lantern pulled Tizzie over on to the deck very roughly.

'Help us, help us, please help us. Let us have some food.'

Tizzie could now hear that the cries of the children were coming from inside the ship. The man with the lantern lifted up a hatch on the deck and growled into the darkness of the hold.

'Shut up you lot. You know there'll be trouble tomorrow if Cap'n Pigleg's sleep is disturbed.'

All went quiet down below.

By the light of the lantern, Tizzie could see that the man was short and stout, with lots of tattoos on his arms. She also saw that he had tattoos covering his whole face and neck. A picture of a mouth with big purple lips and huge white teeth covered his mouth. He looked like a very scary clown.

The tattoo-mouth moved as he spoke. 'Ah, Mr Cudgel, nice to see you've got some more bait for our little expedition.'

'That I have, Purgy, that I have,' answered Mr Cudgel. 'I should think Grunter would hop a long way to eat this one, wouldn't you?' he continued, forcing Tizzie's chin up so Purgy could see her face in the light of the lantern.

The short man grinned. The tattoo-mouth grinned at the same time. Then both men laughed loudly, as if sharing a well-worn joke. Now Tizzie saw that Purgy had no real teeth at all, just a very long tongue with a snake tattooed on it.

'I'll get her into the hold with the others right now, Mr Cudgel.'

'You do that, Purgy. And make sure they all keep as quiet as the moon; the Cap'n 'll be madder 'n Big Red if his sleep is disturbed before we sail in the mornin'?'

'Aye, aye, Mr Cudgel, 'twill be done, just as you say, just as you say.'

Tizzie struggled and waved her arms as Purgy tried to push her down through the hatch.

'Put your feet on the ladder and down you go, girl,' he snarled through pursed lips. 'If you give me any trouble, I'll put you on the Cap'n's bad slave list. Then there'll be *real* trouble, *real* trouble.'

Tizzie didn't want to upset Captain Pigleg; he sounded terrifying, certainly scarier than the dark of the hold.

She reluctantly gave in and put her left foot on the first rung, then her right foot on the second. By the fifth step, her head had gone below the level of the hatch.

Crash!

The heavy wooden cover slammed shut above her and she was in darkness.

# FOURTEEN

# Jack

All Tizzie could hear were the moans and groans and crying and sobbing of lots of children growing louder and louder as she took each step down the ladder.

Finally she stepped off the last rung and felt the soles of her feet touch the cold, wet, wooden floor of the ship's hold. The ship swayed and creaked.

Tizzie jumped as a boy's voice spoke in the darkness.

'You can sit next to me if you like.'

Tizzie's eyes became more used to the dark as she made her way towards the voice, stumbling over other children as she went.

'Sorry... sorry,' she said, each time she trod on someone.

After five or six steps, she could just make out the face of a boy whom she thought was smiling at her.

'Sit down here; it's a good space and there's a rag for a pillow,' said the boy.

Tizzie heard a rattling sound and noticed that he was chained to the hull.

'Thank you,' she said, gratefully.

'Here, I've got half a biscuit saved from the rations,' offered the boy, 'are you hungry?'

It was then that Tizzie realised just how hungry she was.

'Yes I am, but it's your food.'

'That's okay,' said the boy nonchalantly, as he put out his hand and gave her the food. 'We've all got to stick together if we're going to get out of this alive.'

Tizzie took the half a biscuit and stuffed it all in her mouth at once. She immediately regretted that. It was like no biscuit she had ever tasted; all doughy and mouldy. Tizzie swallowed it anyway. She was so hungry and tired and cold, she decided she didn't care about things like that any more.

When Tizzie had stopped munching, the boy spoke again.

'My name is Jack, and I'm from Kernowland.'

'I'm Tizzie.'

'I was thirteen last week, how old are you?'

'Nearly eleven.'

'Where are you from?'

'England.'

'Ah, Angleland. I've never been there,' said Jack.

Tizzie wanted to correct Jack, but thought better of telling him that it was England, not Angleland, that she came from.

She now accepted that she and Louis had somehow come to a very different place through the steaming blue rock in the high cavern at the end of the long windy cave tunnel; but she was not at all ready to try to explain everything to her new friend.

Instead, Tizzie changed the subject.

'Why are you chained up?'

'Because, about three months ago, just after they kidnapped me, I tried to escape. Got three lashes from Gurt as well; the scars on my back have only just healed.'

'Who's Gurt?'

'He's Pigleg's punisher. Hands like shovels. Skin tougher than hide. Eyes that bulge as if his brain's pushing on them.

'Used to be a eunuch protecting the harem of Ali, the Sultan of Sandland. Pigleg freed him in a raid. He's mute too. The story goes that Ali cut out his tongue so he couldn't talk to all the wives in the harem.

'They say that only giants are bigger than Gurt, but I've never seen a real giant. He's twice as tall as me, and round as a barrel.

'Gurt always gives out Pigleg's punishments. Think he enjoys it a lot. He gurgled out loud every time he lashed me.

'They made all the other kids watch as well. Pigleg thinks it's good for discipline.'

Tizzie grimaced, as if she could really feel the whip herself.

She thought Jack must be very brave to stand up to Captain Pigleg and the other pirates, and try to escape.

Tizzie then asked him about something that had been troubling her.

'The man with the tattoos said we're going to Jungleland?'

'That's right. Pigleg's after Grunter, to get his revenge and the reward... and we're the bait.'

'But Mr Cudgel said I might be sold in Sandland as a slave-wife or something.'

'That's what will happen if Big Red doesn't show. He's very clever and if he gets a sniff of a trap he won't take any of us. Or he may get caught and killed while trying to take and eat one of us.

'If he doesn't show, or he gets killed, that's when they'll take us back on board and sell each of us around the wurld to the highest bidder.

'You'd better get some sleep now. We can talk more in the morning.'

Tizzie's mind was racing.

She couldn't even begin to imagine the horror of being eaten slowly by a big red pig, and she had no idea what it would be like to be a slave-wife.

But she didn't want to ask too many questions because Jack might suspect she wasn't from this place. How could she explain that? He surely wouldn't believe her unless she could prove it.

On the other hand, she had a strange feeling that everything would be all right whilst Jack was around. She didn't know quite why, but he somehow made her feel safe.

The other children were quieter now.

Tizzie thought all sorts of thoughts about what might have happened to Louis, and what might happen to her and Jack; but after a while she was too tired to think about anything any more.

She laid her head on the rag pillow, closed her eyes, and was soon asleep.

# FIFTEEN

# Misty

Back at the Polperro Inn, Louis was locked in a cold, dark cellar. He was all on his own, except for a tiny sky-blue mouse, which kept scampering across the stone floor into a beam of yellow light that shone down through a crack in the floorboards of the inn. Louis had never seen a blue mouse before.

Earlier, a man they called 'Scurvy' had bought him for nine crowns.

Louis was petrified of Mr Scurvy. He had mangled ears, which looked as if they had been chewed, and gums which bled so much that his teeth were stained red, and blood oozed from the corner of his mouth in a little trickle that dripped on to his shirt.

The man hadn't taken Louis away immediately, as had happened to Tizzie.

Instead, Melanchol Drym had thrown Louis down some stone steps into the cellar, where he landed on his bad foot, causing the cut from the beach to start bleeding again.

It was a long time that he'd been in there as far as he could work out.

'One thousand and one, one thousand and two…'

He had started counting the seconds, but kept forgetting the last number, so he soon gave that up and tried to sleep with his head resting on a sack of something soft.

But the people in the inn above were still singing and shouting and stomping their feet, and banging their tankards on the wooden tables. There was no chance of any sleep, so Louis watched the mouse, which was now perched on a sack a few feet away, poised to run down the slope and into the beam of light again.

Gradually, the noise above subsided, and the creaky door of the inn banged ever more often as the people left. Louis wondered where they were all going. He imagined them returning to their smuggling houses and pirate ships.

After another while, Louis heard what sounded like a brushing sound. He thought someone must be sweeping up.

Looking up through the crack in the floorboards, he glimpsed the bottom of Mrs Maggitt's petticoats, which swirled from side to side as she swept. The brush on the end of the broom looked like it was made of old twigs and straw.

Just then, a small piece of bread fell through the crack in the wooden floorboards and landed on the cold stone of the cellar floor, right in the middle of the yellow circle made by the beam of light.

Louis was very hungry. He reached out towards the bread, but the mouse ran quickly down the side of the sack and across the floor, grabbing up the bread in its teeth before Louis could get there.

The mouse scurried back up the sack and perched itself triumphantly at the top again. It took the bread between its front paws and began to nibble all around the edges, watching Louis all the while with its wide blue eyes.

A tear began to trickle down Louis' cheek. He was cold and hungry and frightened, in a strange land with no hope of escape or finding Tizzie, and he just wanted his mum to give him a cuddle and read him a bed-time story.

The little blue mouse moved cautiously forwards. As it got closer, Louis was sure he could see a pale blue mist around it. The mouse kept coming, closer and closer, still holding the bread in its mouth.

Then it dropped the bread, stepped backwards, and glanced up at Louis and down at the bread three times, as if to suggest Louis should take it.

Louis snatched up the bread and ate it in one gulp.

Looking at the sky-blue fur of the mouse, Louis whispered, 'I'm going to call you Bluey.'

'*Okay, little man,*' said a squeaky voice in Louis' head, '*but my real name is Misty.*'

Without thinking about how the mouse had spoken to him inside his head, Louis replied aloud.

'All right, I'll call you Misty then.'

With that, Misty came closer again, heading towards Louis' bad foot, which was still stinging terribly.

Louis stayed perfectly still, waiting to see what his tiny new friend would do.

Misty padded up to the sole of Louis' foot, sniffed it, stood on his hind legs and then waggled his whiskers up and down and from side to side.

Louis felt a warm sensation on the bottom of his foot, and the stinging completely stopped. He bent his knee to have a look at it. The cut was gone.

Before Louis could say anything, Misty ran along his leg, clambered up his rag shirt and jumped into the breast pocket.

Louis looked down into the pocket. Misty looked back up at him with his big blue eyes open wide and his whiskers twitching. Louis stared deep into Misty's eyes and now felt the same warm glow all over his body that he had felt on his foot.

'Can you understand me, Misty?' asked Louis.

'*Of course I can,*' said the voice in Louis' head.

Louis was sure the mouse nodded at the same time.

'*The question is: how can you understand me? You don't look like a Rainbow Wizard's apprentice.*'

Louis was just about to ask what Misty meant, when a cloud of dust puffed down from above. Mrs Maggitt was still sweeping. The dust particles were illuminated by the yellow beam of light as they floated down.

'Aaachooo!'

Louis sneezed, loudly.

At that very moment, an object dropped through the crack in the floorboards and clinked and tinkled as it landed and bounced around on the cold stone floor.

# SIXTEEN

## The Golden Key

Misty poked his head out over the top of the shirt pocket to take a look at what had dropped on to the cellar floor.

Louis picked up the small metal object. It was a key. He held the key in the beam of light. It was made of gold.

'Look Misty, it's got strange writing all down one side.'

'*That'll be the Half-Lock Spell that goes with it to make it work,*' said Misty, matter-of-factly inside Louis' head. '*Definitely* not *a Rainbow Wizard's apprentice.*'

Misty suddenly froze and dived into the bottom of the pocket.

'*Please don't let them see me, or they'll kill me; they hate Rainbow Magic.*'

There was a cracking sound as the cellar trapdoor was pulled open. And as the light from above streamed in, Louis quickly dropped the golden key into the pocket with Misty, just before Mr Scurvy looked down on him.

'Get up here now, boy,' he growled, through his clenched, red-stained teeth.

Louis looked up. A drop of blood fell from the corner of Mr Scurvy's mouth and splattered on Louis' forehead.

'Come on, come on, we haven't got all night.'

Louis thought he had better do as he was told. He stood up quickly and climbed the stone steps out of the cellar and in to the inn.

'Hurry, hurry along. The Young Master will be none too pleased if I don't deliver his key to him at the appointed time.'

As he spoke, Scurvy put his hand in a pouch that was hanging around his waist.

His face turned crimson, and his whole head began to wobble as his finger poked through a hole in the bottom of the pouch.

'Where's the key?' he roared, looking accusingly, first at Mr Maggitt, then Mrs Maggitt.

'I don't know what you're talking about, Mr Scurvy,' said Mr Maggitt, shaking his head furiously.

'Nor do I,' said his wife, her bottom lip trembling.

Without thinking, Louis instinctively went to cover his top pocket with his hand. Six eyes glared down at him. Before he could even get to his pocket, Mr Maggitt grabbed Louis' arms and pulled them behind his back.

'So, we've got a little thief, have we?' growled Scurvy. 'The Young Master will sling 'im in irons in Thunder Tower for the rest of 'is life for this.'

Scurvy stretched out his hand and went for Louis' pocket.

Louis didn't care about the key; he wanted to save Misty. Without a concern for the consequences, he bit Mr Scurvy's finger as hard as he could.

'Owww!' screamed Scurvy, putting his bleeding finger in his bloody mouth.

Scurvy scowled, and slapped Louis across the face. Louis stared at him, pursing his lips in defiance.

Mr Scurvy went for the pocket again, but this time grabbed Louis' nose between two fingers of one hand while he put his other hand into the pocket.

'Owww!' screamed Scurvy again, as the same finger was bitten, this time by Misty.

Once more, Mr Scurvy put his sore finger in his mouth for comfort.

Inside the pocket, Louis suddenly felt Misty's whiskers

and wet nose against his chest.

'*I've chewed a hole and I'm going to hide inside your shirt,*' said the now familiar voice inside his head.

Then he felt Misty's claws digging into his skin as the mouse scampered down his body and around his back. Louis felt the coldness of the golden key and the warmth of Misty's body on his spine.

Mr Scurvy went for the pocket again, this time warily pulling at the top of it with one hand whilst holding Louis' nose again with the other.

'There's nothing in there,' he groaned. 'What sort of wizard craft is this?'

'The boy's a spellcaster,' exclaimed Mr Maggitt.

'Gag and bind him quickly before he jinxes us,' shrieked Mrs Maggitt.

'So I shall,' said Mr Scurvy. 'Warlock Warleggan will know what to do with him.'

Moments later, Louis found himself gagged once again, with his hands tied tightly behind his back.

Mr Scurvy grabbed the little tuft of blond hair on the top of Louis' head and tugged on it to make him move towards the door.

'Be sure to tell the Young Master who it was that helped you,' snivelled Mrs Maggitt.

'You can be certain of that, fair lady,' promised Mr Scurvy. 'There may even be a reward after "you know what" happens.'

'Shhh,' said Mr Maggitt, putting his finger over his lips and nodding in Louis' direction, indicating to Mr Scurvy that he shouldn't say another word.

Louis wondered what the 'you know what' was, and when it would happen.

Pulling tighter on Louis' hair, Scurvy grabbed the door

handle and opened the door.

But before he could drag Louis another step, he was stopped in his tracks.

Five long musket barrels were pointed at him, each only a few inches from his nose.

# SEVENTEEN

# Jenny

Tizzie awoke in the hold of *The Revenger* to the insistent sound of a girl's voice.

'Come on, wake up. Wake up!'

Tizzie opened her eyes from her dozing to see the outline of the girl silhouetted against the sunlight as it streamed in through the open hatch above her. She was staring down at Tizzie with her hands on her hips.

'You need to get up and report on deck now,' she warned. 'Captain Pigleg wants to see everybody.'

When her eyes had got more accustomed to the bright sunlight, Tizzie could see the girl more clearly. She had jet-black hair, tied in a ponytail, and a very pretty face. Tizzie guessed the girl was about eleven or twelve.

'Who are you?'

'I'm Jenny, the new cabin girl. Quickly now or the captain will get even more angry. He's already in a very bad mood about something.'

Tizzie looked across at Jack.

In the morning light, she could see he had dark hair and sparkling blue eyes. She felt strange, as if she had perhaps met him before.

Then she realised that he was staring at Jenny.

Tizzie didn't quite know why, but she really didn't like the way Jack was looking at this cabin girl. After all, he was *her* friend, and this girl was one of the pirates, the enemy. Jack shouldn't be looking at her as if he liked her!

Tizzie gently prodded Jack in the ribs to get his attention.

'Let's go before we get in to more trouble,' she said to him, quite bossily.

'Oh, yes, right,' stuttered Jack, but he seemed so confused by Jenny that he tried to get up and move off with his chains still on. He fell back down again.

'Here, let me unlock them,' said Jenny, kindly.

Tizzie watched, getting crosser and crosser as Jenny knelt down and gently took Jack's left foot and unlocked the shackle.

'Ooh, it looks sore,' she said. 'I'll see if I can get you something soothing for it later, when they're not looking.'

'Thanks,' said Jack, still staring at Jenny as if in a trance.

Tizzie seethed. How could her new friend behave like this? Last night she thought he was a hero. Now she wondered if he was a traitor.

Tizzie decided to leave Jack behind, and climbed the wooden steps out of the hold with all the other children.

'Get 'em lined up for the Cap'n, Purgy,' growled Mr Cudgel through clenched teeth and pursed lips, tapping his truncheon arm on his upturned palm as if he was very annoyed about something.

'Right you lot, get in line over here,' boomed Purgy, 'and look lively, the Cap'n's coming.'

The children quickly formed lines on the deck near the bow of the ship. Each line stretched from port to starboard.

It was now that Tizzie noticed for the first time how different all the children were. It was as if there were one child from every country she could imagine.

All the pirates were standing around on the deck, or hanging off the rigging, each grinning and staring expectantly at the children, as if they knew something terrible was going to happen to them.

'They're for it now,' Tizzie heard one say to another.

Then everything went silent.

To Tizzie, it seemed that even the creaking of the ship had stopped for the arrival of the captain. A shiver went down her spine as she heard a sinister sound coming from the stern of the ship.

Click, thud. Click, thud. Click, thud.

The hoof and the foot.

Tizzie knew this was the tell-tale sound of Captain Pigleg. It got louder and louder and louder until the leader of the pirates came into view.

Tizzie couldn't believe her eyes.

# EIGHTEEN

## Dribble the Dust Dog

Dribble was watching Melanchol Drym eating his breakfast. Drym ate cold lumpy porridge every day for every meal. He made it on Monday mornings, in a big pot which had *Drym's Pot* written on the side, and then ate it cold for the rest of the week.

Drym was so mean that he didn't buy any other food at all, and only fed Dribble every other day. Dribble hated cold porridge. He had often wondered what other food tasted like.

'What are you looking at, droopy ears?' sneered Drym. 'It's not your food day until tomorrow, so get out and get on with your work.'

Drym grabbed Spikey and pointed it at the back door of the small dirty house that he lived in alone, just outside the little hamlet of Splatt, near Padstow port.

Dribble did as he was told. As he padded on his short legs towards the door, his big floppy ears dragged along the floor, mopping up the drool that dripped from the corner of his mouth as he went.

Dribble knew his ears were too long, but that was because Drym had always picked him up by them ever since he was a tiny puppy, and they had become stretched.

Now he was thinking back to that time, Dribble growled under his breath. He tried to block the memory out, but he couldn't help remembering the day that Drym had stolen the litter of eight puppies that he'd happened to see in a basket in a cottage garden.

Dribble was such a youngster at the time that his eyes hadn't even opened, and he had never seen his mummy, Dearest; he had only heard her sweet bark. He would never forget that bark.

He longed to find his mummy, as he missed her terribly, and was sure she must be missing him.

Dribble had heard Drym laughing and telling Spikey what he was doing as he had put the other seven puppies, Dribble's three brothers and four sisters, in a big brown sack and thrown them in a stinky pond.

Dribble had smelt the stench of the pond, and heard the splash of the sack in the water, and the yelping and gurgling of his brothers and sisters. Dribble had never forgotten those sounds either.

As Drym carried him away on his smelly old cart, Dribble had heard his mummy's frantic barking in the distance, getting louder and louder.

Since that awful day, he often wondered whether she had heard her puppies crying for help, and if the barking meant she was racing to save them from drowning in the stinky pond.

In actual fact, Dearest had just made it to the pond in time and dived in to rescue her puppies.

But, for Dribble, it was terrible not knowing whether his brothers and sisters had been saved from that dreadful fate, and not a day went by without him thinking about it.

Dribble seethed inside as he thought again about what Drym had done.

'Get a move on, slobber-tongue,' shouted Drym across the room when he saw that Dribble was day-dreaming. 'Lazy good-for-nothing mutt. I sometimes wish I'd kept one of your brothers and sisters instead of you.'

This brought Dribble to his senses, and he growled

again. But it was a low growl. He didn't want to let Drym hear and make him angry.

When he got really furious, Drym kicked poor little Dribble with his pointy shoes and hit him with Spikey. Drym would kick and hit. Dribble would yelp. Drym would laugh out loud and do it again.

So Dribble was very careful not to annoy Drym if he could possibly avoid it.

Dribble was a dust dog. He sifted the mound of rubbish, that Drym piled up at the back of the house, for things that Drym could use or sell. Every day, Drym would collect more rubbish on his cart, and dump it in the back garden for Dribble to sift through. Dribble could hardly keep up.

The mound was now taller than the house, and Dribble got so tired going up and down it every day that he just fell fast asleep in his kennel each night as soon as he had finished work.

Dribble had just started going through the newly arrived rubbish when, high in the sky, he spotted Craw flying towards the house.

Craw was a carrier crow, who worked for Wendron, the wrinkled witch.

# NINETEEN

# Prong

Louis looked up at the five long gun barrels pointed at Mr Scurvy.

'Stand fast in the name of the King,' ordered a straight-backed young officer who wore a black cape and sat on a magnificent white horse. 'Sergeant Stout, escort His Highness to his mount if you'd be so kind.'

'Yes sir,' answered a tough-looking man with a thick moustache. Louis noticed he was wearing three gold stripes on the arm of his black and gold shirt. His black and gold kilt flapped in the breeze, and he wore shiny black boots.

The sergeant walked towards Louis, who didn't quite know what to do. Who is 'His Highness', he wondered. He couldn't see anyone who looked like a King.

Just at that moment, Louis heard a voice he recognised.

'Protocol demands proper introductions before we proceed, I'm sure you'll agree, lieutenant.'

It was Gwithian Sand, waddling towards him as fast as his short legs would allow. The little man seemed to be trying to get to Louis quicker than the sergeant, and he winked and smiled as he approached.

Meanwhile, the officer nodded deferentially, replying: 'Of course, of course. I stand corrected, sir.'

When he got up close, Mr Sand quickly loosened Louis' gag, speaking softly and hurriedly as he freed the boy's hands from their bonds.

'Please trust me, young man. Let me do the talking. Don't tell them where you are really from. Quickly now, whisper me your name.'

Louis liked Mr Sand and did trust him.

'Louis,' he whispered.

Mr Sand wheeled around and addressed the young officer on the white horse once more.

'Lieutenant Liskeard of the Launceston Lancers, may I present His Royal Highness, Louis, a Prince of Forestland.'

'I and my men are at your service, Your Highness,' said the Lieutenant, bowing as he spoke.

Louis was very surprised to see the great white horse bow at the same time as the young officer.

All the other soldiers – Louis counted about twelve of them – bowed to Louis as well, except the five who still had their musket barrels pointed at Mr Scurvy. They didn't move an inch.

When he had stopped bowing, Sergeant Stout stood to attention and spoke in a clipped voice.

'My pleasure to escort 'is 'ighness to 'is mount.'

Louis glanced at Mr Sand, who nodded his head quickly up and down a couple of times, which Louis took to mean he should follow Sergeant Stout.

As Louis walked behind the sergeant towards a small sturdy-looking silver pony, he heard an excited voice in his head which definitely wasn't Misty because it was much deeper and louder.

'*Oh yes. I knew it would happen one day. It's my destiny. I'm going to be a royal pony at last. Better do this right.*'

As he heard the voice, Louis saw the silver pony bend all four of its legs at the knees so that its tummy rested on the ground.

Louis had seen camels bend down like that so someone could get on to them, but never a pony.

Most boys might have been worried at the thought of

getting on a pony, but Louis had been riding for two years at home and had already been on a much bigger horse than this mount.

'This is Prong, Your Highness,' said Sergeant Stout, 'a fine example of the famous Kernish Tor Pony. He's strong, swift, and proud to serve the King.'

'Thank you, Sergeant,' said Louis, a bit condescendingly with his nose in the air, trying to behave as he thought a real prince might.

'*Obviously a prince with fine royal breeding*,' said the deep voice in Louis' head, as he put his right leg over the brown saddle and fixed his feet in the stirrups like an experienced rider.

'*Now, if I can just get off to a good start and get up smoothly…*'

As Louis heard this, Prong took his front hooves out from under him, put them flat on the cobbles and raised his chest off the ground. Then he slowly and smoothly pushed up his back legs until all four legs were straight.

Louis was hardly wobbled at all by the movement.

'*There, not bad even if I say so myself*,' said the same voice.

Now Louis was certain who it was that was speaking inside his head. It was Prong.

'Very good, Prong, very good,' he said encouragingly, knowing that Prong would love to hear him say that.

'*Brilliant. He likes me already*,' heard Louis, as he patted Prong's neck.

Lieutenant Liskeard's orders made Louis pay attention.

'On with the business at hand, Sergeant, over to you.'

'Sheviok Scurvy, I arrest you in the name of the King, for slaving, an offence against the Crown and Kingdom of Kernowland.'

Louis saw Scurvy's head drop. The constant trickle of blood from his mouth began dripping on to his boots instead of his shirt.

Then Louis watched as Mr and Mrs Maggitt were marched around from the back of the building by two soldiers.

'Ah, the Maggitts. We've been hoping to catch you two in the act for years,' said Lieutenant Liskeard, 'and now we've got you red-handed. Sergeant, if you please.'

Sergeant Stout continued with his duty.

'Malpas and Mawla Maggitt, I arrest you in the name of the King, for slaving, an offence against the Crown and Kingdom of Kernowland.'

'And where is the young princess, sister of Prince Louis?' enquired Mr Sand.

'S... s... sold, sir. We're s... so s... s... sorry,' stuttered Mrs Maggitt. 'We was made to do it. Made, we was.'

'Quiet woman,' scolded her husband.

'Sold to whom?' boomed Mr Sand, in a voice that seemed very loud and commanding, coming, as it did, from such a small body.

'Pigleg,' snarled Scurvy, looking up and showing all his red-stained teeth and bleeding gums in a big smirk.

Louis could see from their faces that everyone thought this was very bad news; very bad news indeed.

He hoped Tizzie was all right.

# TWENTY

## Captain Pigleg

Still trembling, Tizzie stared at Captain Pigleg. The leader of the pirates was tall and lean with red curly hair and a red curly beard, which were both frizzed out in all directions, making his head look three times normal size.

His head was on fire! Wisps of red smoke rose into the air.

Captain Pigleg had a red leather patch over his left eye, and a gleaming gold hook in place of his left hand. He wore a red coat, with lots of gold buttons, which was so long it nearly touched the deck.

The coat was open, and Tizzie could see Pigleg's cutlass stuck in his belt, its red-jewelled hilt gleaming in the sunlight.

She also glimpsed the blood-stained bone and hoof that replaced his lower leg. It was totally gruesome.

As the captain took a couple more paces forward, she now saw that he had four round gold earrings in his left ear. From his right ear, a red ruby in the shape of pig dangled on a long gold earchain, so that the pig rested on the front of his shoulder.

Pigleg played with the ruby pig with his fingers for what seemed like ages. Then he suddenly let go of it, and spit flew out of his mouth in all directions as he spoke.

'Sohhh… hungry are yee!?'

All the children jumped at once.

'Crying and asking for more food in the middle o' the night and disturbing me sleep, were yeee!?'

Pigleg's eye squinted and searched along the lines.

Tizzie saw that all the children looked at the deck at once, as if none of them wanted the captain to look at them. She quickly did the same.

'Well, werrr yeeee!?' boomed the captain again, even louder than before.

The children maintained their silence, still looking at the deck.

'Answer the Cap'n,' barked Mr Cudgel, tapping his truncheon arm on his palm even more menacingly than before.

'Aye, aye, sir, Captain Pigleg,' said all the children at once.

Except Tizzie, who joined in but was a little later than the others. The 'Pigleg' part of what she said came out after all the other children had stopped answering.

Jack looked across at her with compassion in his eyes, as if he knew something awful was going to happen to her.

Click, thud, click, thud, click, thud.

Captain Pigleg took three paces forward so that he was standing right in front of Tizzie.

She looked down at the deck, shaking uncontrollably. When was this nightmare going to end?

Pigleg put the point of his hook under her chin and pulled her head up so that she had to look at him.

Then he bent down so that his mouth was just inches from her eyes. The ten gold rings in his lips, and the five gold pins in his nostrils, and the three gold studs in his tongue all moved together as he spoke.

'Do I detect insubordination in the ranks, shipmates?' he yelled, splattering spit all over Tizzie's face as he did so.

'Aye, aye, sir, Cap'n Pigleg,' shouted his crew in complete unison, as if they were well-drilled navy men.

The sound rang loudly in Tizzie's ears.

'I can feel a lashin' comin' on,' scowled Pigleg. 'That'll be a lesson for all o' them.

'Have a man fetch Gurt from his slumber if ye'd be so kind, Mr Cudgel,' he instructed, glancing up at his first mate before staring back at Tizzie. 'And make sure he brings Lasher with 'im.'

'Aye, aye, Cap'n,' said Mr Cudgel. 'Purgy, you heard the Cap'n. Get Gurt.'

'That I will, Mr Cudgel, that I will,' said Purgy, glancing over his shoulder to give Tizzie a nasty smile with his tattoo-mouth, as he moved towards the cabin house.

Gurt.

Lasher.

Lesson.

A jumble of alarm bells rang even louder in Tizzie's head. It quickly dawned on her that the lashing was going to be for her.

This was finally all too much for Tizzie. She could feel everyone's eyes on her. She felt dizzy and short of breath. The ship started to spin.

Suddenly, everything inside her head went black.

# TWENTY-ONE

## The Tattered Map

'Get them prisoners in the gaol wagon, and look lively!'

The gruff voice rang loudly in Louis' ears as he watched the soldiers carry out Sergeant Stout's instruction to put Scurvy and the Maggits in a strong-looking cart. The cart had huge wheels at the sides, and a big iron cage attached on top. Two heavy brown horses were harnessed at the front.

'Right men, back to Truro,' ordered Lieutenant Liskeard. 'The King awaits his royal visitor at Kernow Castle, and we must raise the alarm to rescue the princess. We'll stop just once on the way, at Eden Valley, to rest the horses and eat.'

Lifting his arm to signal everyone to follow him, Lieutenant Liskeard led the way on his big white horse.

'Forward, Blanco.'

Louis and Mr Sand – who was riding a mud-brown, short-legged, shaggy-haired old donkey called Dodger – were next in line.

Then came Sergeant Stout on foot, then the gaol wagon, and then all the other soldiers marching along at the rear.

Mr Sand showed Louis the landscape of Kernowland as they went along.

'Look, Your Highness,' or 'look, Prince Louis,' he would say when pointing things out. Louis liked this game. He liked being treated as a prince and told important things. He listened attentively to all he was being taught.

'There is an ancient language called *Kernewek*,' Mr

Sand informed Louis, 'which is still spoken in parts of Kernowland.

'Lots of words in this tongue begin with short three-letter words like *Tre, Pol,* or *Pen* – as do many names of people – and there is an old saying, which all Kernow children learn from an early age: "By Tre, Ros, Car, Lan, Pol, and Pen, Ye may know most Kernow Men".'

This started Louis thinking about Kernewek words, and a question popped into his head: 'What does "tor" mean?'

'It means "hill",' was Mr Sand's answer.

'So Prong is a *hill* pony,' said Louis, to a nodding smile from Mr Sand.

'*And a rather handsome, dashing, swift one, fit to carry a prince,*' said the proud voice in Louis' head.

After a few hours' travelling, Lieutenant Liskeard raised his arm, and the troop halted. The officer straightened his legs in his stirrups and rose up a little from his saddle as he shouted his orders to the back of the line.

'Right men, make ready for the descent in to Eden Valley.'

The soldiers began tying any loose items to themselves or the horses, and made sure the cage was securely attached to the gaol wagon. Surveying the steep slopes, Louis could see why they were taking such precautions; it was going to be a rough ride.

Straight ahead, down in the hollow of the deep valley, he saw two huge white domes, just like those Tizzie had shown him in the car. The domes were surrounded by trees and plants and flowers of all the colours of the rainbow. An array of flags fluttered in the wind.

Louis stared at the strange and wonderful sight before him, but before he could ask any questions, Mr Sand pulled a piece of folded parchment from inside his jacket.

'Here, Prince Louis,' he said, unfolding the parchment as he spoke, 'whilst we're waiting, let me show you something about map reading and navigation; the art and science of finding your way around.'

Louis looked at the parchment. It was very old, with tattered corners and lots of creases, as if it had been used often.

On the parchment was drawn a map with the word *Kernowland* written in large squiggly letters above it.

In the top left-hand corner was a long arrow, which divided a circle in half and pointed upwards to a very large letter *N*. Around the circle, in clockwise order after the *N*, were three smaller letters: *E*, *S*, and *W*.

'One of the easiest ways to confirm your position is to survey the terrain and then see if there is anything that you can recognise on the map,' began Mr Sand. 'Look around; what can you see?'

Louis looked. To his left, far off in the distance, he saw the ocean. To his right, there were more hills, stretching out for miles. But, of course, the most obvious feature was straight in front of him, down at the bottom of the deep valley: two huge white domes.

He explained what he saw to Mr Sand.

'Very good observation, Louis,' praised Mr Sand. 'So, if we look around at the terrain, and then at the map, we can be fairly sure that we're near the place marked *Eden Valley*.'

Map reading is easy, thought Louis... until Mr Sand continued.

'However, as well as knowing where we are, it is often very important that we know where we're going and how to get there.

'That's why, for good navigation, as well as a map we need a special instrument.'

# TWENTY-TWO

## Craw

Dribble thought there must be something important going on for Wendron to be sending a message to Drym.

He padded to the back door of the house, which was still slightly ajar. Nudging the door open a little more with his nose, the dust dog put his head just far enough into the room so that he could see and hear and smell what was going on.

Craw flew in through an open window with a small piece of parchment tied to his leg by a length of string. Dribble watched as Craw headed straight for the table.

Unfortunately for the bird, a dollop of Drym's cold, slippery porridge was right where he landed, and he skidded straight off the end of the table, hitting the back of a chair and landing in a heap on the hard seat.

Drym's snigger became a sneer as he grabbed Craw by the throat.

'Crorrrhhh!' choked Craw, as Drym held him up at arms length with one hand, and tore at the string with the other.

'My dream is coming true, oh yes it is,' smirked Drym, pulling at the string so savagely that it cut into Craw's leg before snapping and allowing the note to drop to the floor.

'Crorrrhhh!' shrieked Craw again, as Drym released his grip on the crow's throat, dropping the poor bird so quickly that he had no chance to flap his wings before crashing back down on the hard seat of the chair.

'Crorrrhhh!'

Owww. That must have hurt, thought Dribble.

Oblivious to Craw's discomfort, Drym picked up the parchment, drew Spikey from his belt and put the pointed stick on another chair.

He began to talk to the stick as if it were a person.

'Look what we've got, Spikey. I wonder if it's the news we've been waiting for.'

Craw, who had now regained his composure, and was perched on the chair back, looked confused.

Dribble wasn't confused though. He knew that Spikey was Drym's imaginary friend. In fact, the stick was his *only* friend and he talked to it all the time.

Dribble listened closely as Drym read the note on the parchment aloud to Spikey. Like lots of writing in Kernowland, and all over Erthwurld, it took the form of a verse.

> *I have heard the word from our mutual friend,*
> *Midsummer morn will herald Kernowland's end.*
> *The King and the Kernowfolk will soon have to pay,*
> *For then 'twill be time for Darkness Day.*

It sounds like something terrible is going to happen, thought Dribble anxiously.

And midsummer is only two days away.

# TWENTY-THREE

## The Kernow Compass

Mr Sand fumbled inside his shirt for a thin, flat, round object hanging on a piece of cord around his neck. It was about the size of a pocket watch, and he held it in his palm to show Louis as he spoke.

'This is a Kernow compass.'

'As you can see, it's circular and there are lots of dots, called "points", all around the circumference; three-hundred-and-sixty of them to be precise. They show all the possible directions in which we could travel. The four main points are: *North, East, South,* and *West.*'

Louis looked. The four main points were marked on the face of the compass with letters: *N, E, S, W.*

'The compass has a magnetic metal needle inside, which is balanced on a pin, so that it can swing around freely,' continued Mr Sand.

'We take advantage of the natural fact that the needle always wants to point to the North Pole in Snowland. If we line up the point of the needle with the *N* marker on the compass, we know which way is north and we can then be sure of all the other directions as well.'

Mr Sand could see Louis looked a bit puzzled, so he explained further.

'To make things easier when we're learning to navigate, we always like to face north first, making sure we hold the map so that the big letter *N* is in the top left-hand corner.'

Being very careful to keep the needle and the *N* together on the compass, Mr Sand then turned Louis and himself around so that they were both facing north, with Louis holding the map open.

'As you can see, both the map *and* the compass are confirming what we thought. The needle is pointing north towards the hills in front of us, which means that the sea is in the south behind us, and Eden Valley is a little bit to the west on our left, which we know is correct because we can see it!'

To finish the map reading lesson, Mr Sand asked some more questions in order to make sure his pupil had understood.

'So, Prince Louis, in relation to our current position, roughly what point on the compass is Polperro, where we started from?'

'East, on our right,' said Louis, fairly confident that he was correct, because he could see the town marked on the southern coast in the lower right-hand corner of the map.

'Very good, and which way have we had to travel to get to Eden Valley?'

'West,' said Louis, now certain of his answer because he could see that west was the opposite way to east.

'So,' continued Mr Sand, 'we've come from the east on the right of the map, and travelled west towards the left of the map to arrive at Eden Valley, a place which is a few miles inland from the south coast at the bottom of the map.'

Louis nodded as Mr Sand spoke, to show he understood what his teacher was saying.

'When we've eaten and we leave Eden Valley, which way will we have to head to Truro?' asked Mr Sand, to make doubly sure his pupil was following everything.

'West,' said Louis.

'Very good,' commended Mr Sand, with a beaming smile. 'You've done exceedingly well with your first map reading and navigation lesson.'

'But what if we didn't have a compass?' asked Louis, sensibly.

'Very good question. We would use the sun to help us. We know that the sun rises in the east and sets in the west. And we know that it is midday now because the sun is directly above us. So, logically, if we follow the sun all afternoon until it sets, we will travel west and head towards Truro.'

'But what if it's night-time and there is no sun?'

'Excellent question. When it's dark, we make use of the faraway suns in the night sky, the stars.'

Louis was fascinated by all he had learned about map reading and navigation using landmarks and a compass, and the sun and the stars. He thought it would be great to be able to find his way around like this by himself.

As if reading Louis' thoughts, Mr Sand then removed the compass from around his neck and handed it to Louis along with the old and tattered parchment map.

'Here, Prince Louis,' he said warmly. 'You now know how to use these navigation tools, and they could come in very useful when we begin the rescue of your sister. But, as with all tools, you will need to practice if you are to become good at using them. So you may as well start right away.'

'Thank you, Mr Sand,' beamed Louis, absolutely delighted with his new map and compass.

'Right, navigation lesson over,' said Mr Sand, smiling broadly and obviously very happy that Louis was so pleased with his gifts.

'Now, let's get down that hill to Eden Valley for some food.'

'Yes,' agreed Louis, 'I'm hungry.'

But as they all stumbled their way slowly down the steep hill, Louis became increasingly worried by a thought that just would not go away.

Perhaps the carnivorous plants would be hungry too.

# TWENTY-FOUR

## Drym's Dripping Dungeon

Having overheard his master telling Spikey what was on the note from Wendron, Dribble listened even more intently as he watched the dastardly dustman slowly rubbing his bony, grey hands together, full of glee.

'At last, I can prepare my dungeon for its real purpose. If we help with the invasion on Darkness Day, the Young Master has promised to put us in charge of child slavery. We'll make a fortune, Spikey. Oh yes we will.

'We'll gather up all those little Kernowkids who drop litter on purpose and laugh at us behind our backs, and we'll put them in our dungeon and hold them there until every last one is sold to the pirates and slave traders. We'll sell them all. Oh yes we will.

'Drip, drip, drip on their little heads, Spikey. We'll see how happy and noisy they are after they've shivered for a whole week with icy cold water plopping down on them all day and all night in my dripping dungeon. Oh yes we will.'

Drym was so greedy and possessive, he labelled and tagged everything he owned. He'd even put a sign above his dungeon which read *Drym's Dungeon*.

The nasty dustman had been sifting through the rubbish for years to find out things about the children in Kernowland, including all their secrets.

Dribble had often wondered why Drym was collecting the names of all the Kernowkids, and writing details about each of them in a book of things he had to do, which had

*Drym's Diary* inscribed on the front cover.

Now the little dog knew the answer. The more information Drym had about the children, the more he could sell them for.

Dribble couldn't just let Drym get away with his traitorous plotting against Kernowland, and he especially didn't want any of the children to be put in the dripping dungeon and sold as slaves.

Dribble loved Kernowkids. They always patted him and stroked him when Drym was not looking because they knew his plight as Drym's dust dog, and felt sorry for him.

Dribble knew the time had come to do something to help Kernowland and save the Kernowkids from slavery.

But what could he do?

He couldn't fight Drym because Drym had Spikey on his side. And he couldn't speak words to tell anyone.

Then Dribble had a realisation. Of course, all the evidence was already written down in a book! If he could just get hold of *Drym's Diary*, he could take it to Clevercloggs.

Dribble had often overheard people say that Clevercloggs was the wisest mind in Kernowland. He had been alive so long and done so many things that they came from far and wide just to listen to him talk about anything and everything. The old gnome, whom everybody revered, would surely know what to do.

Dribble watched as Drym copied Wendron's note into his diary and then put the grey-coloured book away in a drawer, which had *Drym's Drawer* scratched on the front.

Drym locked the drawer, made sure it was secure, and then put the key under the cushion of his favourite armchair.

I must get the diary, resolved Dribble. But how?

# TWENTY-FIVE

## Prince Louis

Lieutenant Liskeard had successfully led everyone down the steep hillside into Eden Valley without incident. They made camp in front of the two big white domes.

Louis was very happy they'd stopped for a rest and a meal; he was very tired and hadn't eaten for ages.

Most of the soldiers made their way to the food hall, but four stayed behind to guard the prisoners who remained in the gaol wagon, having been handed some food and drink through the bars.

Louis started to follow the soldiers who were going to lunch, but Mr Sand took his arm and made it clear he wanted to talk to him. From the look on the little man's face, it concerned something important.

'Apologies, Your Highness. I know you're hungry, but we have to talk further and dress you properly before you meet any other people.

'The soldiers understand you were kidnapped and dressed in those rags by your captors, but we don't want to arouse suspicion amongst the ordinary Kernowfolk.'

Mr Sand walked on, beckoning Louis to follow him as he headed for a huge tree with roots that ran above the ground.

Louis approached the tree, and sat down on one of the roots next to Mr Sand, who began talking very quietly.

'Now, no one can hear what we're saying, not even the animals.'

Misty can hear, thought Louis, as he felt the little warm mouse rummaging about inside his shirt with the cold key. But he's my friend so that's okay.

'Have you any questions?' asked Mr Sand. 'Only it would be good to get some things straight before you talk to anyone else in Kernowland.'

'How did you know where to find me?' asked Louis.

'When I came out of the cave, I climbed up the cliffs and just happened to look back. Well, you can imagine my utter surprise to see you and your sister on the beach. I had no idea that you would guess the password and follow me here to Kernowland.'

'Did you see the giant crabs chasing us?'

'Yes, they serve the King, protecting the Crystal Pool.'

'Would they eat people if they caught them?'

'Well actually, no, the climbing crabs are under instructions to hold trespassers in their pincers, until they are arrested by the soldiers. But they have been known to squeeze people a bit too hard; one or two have even had bones cracked, which is very unfortunate.'

'They're pretty scary,' said Louis, remembering back to his experience on the beach. 'Did you see me fall over?'

'Yes, and I saw you climb the cliff.'

'And did you see the rope man with the grey skin?'

'Yes. And I saw him carry you off in his cart. But I was too far away to help. I quickly organised someone whom I could trust to follow the cart, a choughateer called Perry Perranporth.'

'What's a choughateer?'

'One of our brave and dashing airborne defence fighters. They fly on giant choughs, which are large black birds with red beaks and red feet.'

'I knew I saw a man on a giant bird when we came out of the cave,' said Louis.

'That's right. It must have been Perry you saw. He and

his skymount, Chock, were on a border reconnaissance flight. I signalled to Perry and he landed nearby. I gave him instructions to follow you and report back to me. It was no surprise that you ended up at the Polperro Inn.

'When Perry came back to tell me the news, I had already told the King all about you and your sister. He is very kind and was concerned that we'd drawn you into trouble in Kernowland.

'We made a plan to say you are from Forestland, which is a long way away, in the far north east. Very few Kernowfolk have ever been there. The people have golden hair, too, so that just seemed a good place to choose as your homeland.'

'But why am I a prince?' asked Louis.

'There had to be a reason why the King wanted to see you,' answered Mr Sand. 'So making you a prince was the best we could think of quickly. If anyone asks, you are a distant cousin of the King, and therefore a member of the Royal Family of Kernowland.'

'What's going to happen to the grey man with the sausage dog?' asked Louis.

'From the description, we're pretty sure it's a man called Drym,' replied Mr Sand. 'A troop of Lancers has been sent to arrest him at his house in the hamlet of Splatt.'

'Yes, Drym, that was his name,' remembered Louis.

'We've suspected him of kidnapping and selling Kernowkids for a long time,' added Mr Sand.

'And what will happen to Mr and Mrs Maggitt, and Mr Scurvy?'

'They'll be put in Bodmin Gaol, along with Drym. What with being caught in the act of kidnapping, they should all be in there for a very long time.'

'*And good riddance to the lot of them,*' said the

squeaky voice in Louis' head, as he felt Misty move back into the top pocket of his ragged shirt.

Then Louis remembered Dribble.

'What about Drym's dog? Will he be in trouble too?'

'That depends on whether he was part of the gang. He'll be interviewed by Yellawell, the Rainbow Wizard responsible for Yellow Magic. The Yellow Wizard can talk to animals, by hearing their thoughts.'

'*And that's the truth,*' said the squeaky voice in Louis' head.

For some reason, Louis didn't think it was the right time to tell Mr Sand that he too could hear the thoughts of animals as words in his head. He'd save that for later.

Instead, he asked the big question that was on his mind.

'Will we be able to get back to see Mum and Dad?'

'Oh yes, yes,' assured Mr Sand. 'When we've found your sister, you can both go back home through the Crystal Pool. All you need is the password to go back the other way.'

'What's the password?'

'If I tell you now, you may let it slip to the wrong person by mistake. Or, if you are captured, they may force you to say it. Who knows what would happen if someone like Melanchol Drym or Captain Pigleg got hold of the password and used the Crystal Pool to get into your world. Makes me shudder to think of it. Probably best if I tell you when the time comes.'

Louis agreed. He wanted to know the password but he wasn't sure he could keep it secret if he was captured by Mr Drym again.

# TWENTY-SIX

## Drym's Diary

Since learning that an invasion of Kernowland was planned for midsummer's morning by a group of treacherous plotters and traitors, Dribble had been able to think of little else.

Midsummer's morning was only two days away. Time was running out, and the little dust dog knew he had to act quickly. He had to get *Drym's Diary* and take the evidence to Clevercloggs so that the alarm could be raised.

But Drym had locked Dribble outside to work while he slept, so it wasn't going to be easy.

Drym had been asleep since lunch, and Dribble was listening to his master's snores through the open window.

Now was his chance. He jumped up at the window and managed to get his front paws on the ledge, whilst desperately scraping his back paws against the wall in an attempt to push himself up and into the house.

Just as he thought the plan was working, and he was going to make it, he fell to the ground.

'Pumfff.'

The fall knocked the wind out of him.

Then Dribble had another idea.

When he had been sifting the rubbish earlier, he had seen one of the mini-trampolines which the wealthy ladies of Kernowland bounced on as part of their exercise routines. Most of the ladies only did the exercises for a while, then got bored and threw the trampolines away. Drym was always bringing them back in his cart.

Dribble found the trampoline, dragged it down from halfway up the rubbish pile, and placed it under the window.

Then he climbed right to the top of the mound and ran down it as fast as he could, jumped on to the trampoline and, 'boing', he bounced right up into the air and through the window.

But there was a problem.

Dribble had given himself so much forward momentum that, when he landed, he found himself sliding along the slippery stone floor, straight towards the pointed shoes of his snoring master.

As he was sliding, Dribble was panic stricken, knowing full well that Drym would kick him and beat him and starve him for days if he was found in the house when he was supposed to be working.

The little dust dog desperately twisted his long body sideways to try to stop himself bashing into Drym, whilst at the same time pushing hard on the floor with his paws. Somehow, just before he got to Drym's legs, he stopped.

Dribble's heart was racing but he knew what he had to do. Get that key from under the cushion.

But there was another problem. The key was under the very cushion on which Drym was now sitting.

Dribble knew he had to risk it. He nuzzled his nose under the cushion.

Drym stirred.

Dribble stopped, and waited.

Drym was still asleep.

Dribble nuzzled in again.

Drym stirred again, this time smacking his lips loudly.

Dribble scampered behind another chair, fearful that his master would awaken.

He looked out from behind the chair.

Drym was still asleep and had now moved to one side slightly.

This is my chance, thought Dribble, silently approaching the cushion once more.

One last nuzzle, just a bit further... got it!

Dribble padded quietly over to *Drym's Drawer* with the key in his mouth. He put it in the lock and twisted it with his teeth.

Click.

He heard the lock go.

It sounded very loud, but Melanchol Drym didn't awaken, he just breathed heavily.

Dribble pulled the drawer open slowly. It squeaked every inch of the way.

Drym spluttered and shifted on his chair, this time mumbling under his breath.

Dribble ran back behind the other chair, sure that he'd woken Drym this time.

But Drym didn't stir.

Dribble moved silently back to the drawer, put his paws on the front of it and picked up *Drym's Diary* in his mouth, slobbering profusely as he took the book in his teeth. A large gobbet of saliva dropped on to the floor.

Dribble turned and moved across the room, his ears mopping the saliva along the floor in a tell-tale trail as he headed for the front door... and freedom.

The daring little dachshund had always wondered whether he'd be able to open this door by stretching up on his hind legs. Now was his chance to try.

Luckily, his body was just long enough so that he was just tall enough to push up the latch and open the door with his nose.

Phew, made it.

Dribble sighed to himself with relief.

When outside, he decided not to shut the door for fear of waking Drym. Instead, he just left it wide open and set off down the road towards Washaway Wood, the home of Clevercloggs, the wise old gnome.

What Dribble didn't see was Craw watching everything in sly silence from a perch on top of Drym's house.

# TWENTY-SEVEN

## The Cape and the Kaski

After he had answered some more of Louis' questions, Mr Sand opened a leather saddle-bag and produced a package. It was wrapped in cloth and tied with string. He held the package out in front of him.

'Here, Your Highness,' he whispered, with a wink and a beaming smile. 'Clothes befitting a Prince who is just about to meet a King.'

Louis undid the string and held up the garments. They were the black and gold shirt, jacket, and trousers of a Kernish Army officer's uniform.

'As a cousin of the King, you are entitled to wear that uniform and expect all the privileges which come with it,' said Mr Sand, as if he was saying something very important.

'Black and gold are the colours of the King. The Royal Crest on the jacket shows all who meet you that you are to be treated as a Prince of Kernowland.'

Louis went behind the tree and changed his ragged clothes for the smart uniform, keeping his swimming shorts on underneath.

He put on the black shirt, taking care to transfer Misty and the key into the top left pocket. Then he put on the black jacket and did up the gold buttons as fast as he could.

Pulling on the black trousers, he noticed that each leg had a thumb-thick, gold stripe down the outside.

Louis went around to the front of the tree and showed his new uniform to Mr Sand.

Shaking his head as he looked at Louis' bare feet, Mr

Sand handed him some socks and a pair of shiny black boots. Louis sat down to put these on and then stood up to attention.

'Every inch a soldier-prince,' exclaimed Mr Sand, with another smile. 'Except for your Kernow Cape.'

With that, Mr Sand handed Louis a black cape just like the one that Lieutenant Liskeard was wearing. It had a white cross on the back.

'That is the Flagsign of Kernow,' informed Mr Sand. 'It signifies the Light of Good shining through the darkness of all that is bad.'

'What are these words?' asked Louis, pointing to the letters underneath the cross.

'*Onen hag Oll*,' pronounced Mr Sand proudly. 'That's Kernewek for *One and All*, the ancient motto of Kernowland.

'It means that if we *All* stand together as *One*, nothing can conquer us. And that has been true for centuries.'

'Cool,' said Louis, as Mr Sand wrapped the cape around him.

'You'll find this useful as well,' beamed Mr Sand, handing Louis a small green object and a brown leather sheath attached to a thin leather belt. 'It's a survival knife which has been given Erth Magic properties by Grenlapp, the Green Wizard. It's called a Kernish Army Survival Knife, or "Kaski" for short.'

Louis looked at the Kaski. There were lots of small blades and tools in slots and housings in the handle. He opened some of the blades and pulled out some of the tools; a little saw-blade, one shaped like a tiny screwdriver, a long sharp knife-blade and lots more.

'What's Erth Magic?' asked Louis as he snapped back the blades.

'All the magic to do with the Erth: plants, soil, rocks, and stones. The Green Wizard is in charge of it.'

'So is this a magic knife?' asked Louis.

'Well, each of the Kaski's blades has magic properties that help you survive when exposed to the wild nature of the wurld,' answered Mr Sand. 'But you must know how to use them, or else it's just an ordinary survival knife. The instructions are on the back of the belt. Remind me to tell you more later, because a prince of Kernowland will be expected to know how to use a Kaski.'

Louis put his special new survival knife in its brown leather sheath and buckled the thin leather belt around his waist.

# TWENTY-EIGHT

## The Kernow Catapult

'Now you need a weapon to defend yourself,' said Mr Sand, reaching down into the leather saddle-bag once more.

'Nothing finer than the Kernow Catapult.'

'A catapult,' sighed Louis, letting his disappointment show a bit more than he wanted to. 'Can't I have a gun?'

'A gun!' said Mr Sand, sounding very surprised indeed. 'No real prince would want to carry a gun.'

His voice softened as he saw Louis' head drop. 'But then you aren't from here, are you? I nearly forgot for a moment, seeing you in that uniform.

'You should know that, for centuries, the Kernow Catapult has been the weapon of choice for all young warriors under the age of eleven in Kernowland.

'On their eleventh birthday, they move on to the Kernow Crossbow, until they are eighteen, when they normally have the strength to use the Kernbow, which is a mightily special weapon indeed.'

'But isn't a gun much better?' asked Louis.

Mr Sand gave him another stern look.

'Many in the rest of Erthwurld think so,' he continued, as he handed Louis a small wooden catapult. 'Progress, they call it.

'But, believe me, if you learn to use this ancient weapon of the Old Ways properly, you will be more than a match for any enemy with any gun anywhere in Erthwurld.'

Louis took the catapult Mr Sand handed him.

'You see this,' said the little man earnestly, twanging

the thick stretchy band that was attached to each end of the catapult's fork, 'this will fire the ammunition, small coloured stones called "cataballs", faster than the speed of sound. So be careful.'

Mr Sand handed Louis a small brown sack and a long leather belt. The belt had coloured leather pouches sewn all along it.

Louis held the belt whilst he opened the sack. Inside, there were different coloured stones, each about the size of a marble.

'Now, first we need to put the cataballs in the ammunition belt,' instructed Mr Sand, as Louis helped his teacher put the coloured stones in the little pouches.

'We call the ammunition "ammo" for short. Red balls in the red pouches, orange balls in the orange pouches. That's it; you're getting the idea, Louis... I mean Your Highness, mustn't forget, must I?'

When they had put all the red, orange, yellow, green, blue, indigo, and violet cataballs in their same-coloured pouches on the belt, Mr Sand said: 'Right, time to put it on.'

Louis tried to put the ammo belt around his waist. It was far too long.

'No, no,' smiled Mr Sand. 'It goes over your shoulder and diagonally down across your chest, like this. Then you put the cape over the top.'

'Why are their so many different coloured balls?' asked Louis as he put on the cape.

'Different cataballs are for different purposes. Red is for making holes in things like rocks or trees, or, if you really have to, anything attacking you. Orange is for explosions. And so on. The instructions are on the other side of the ammo belt.'

Louis screwed up his face as if he were a bit sceptical

about the supposed power of the Kernow Catapult and its ammunition. He thought it looked like a toy, not a proper weapon.

Mr Sand noticed his expression. 'As with all things in life, the proof is in the pudding, young man.'

He then showed Louis how to use the catapult.

'Now, simply take one of the red balls, put it in the firing leather in the middle of the stretchy band, pull back hard and...'

Ffffzzzzzzzzzzzzzzzzzzzzzzzzz!

Before Mr Sand had a chance to say another word, Louis had let go of the band.

'Nooooo, you're supposed to aim it carefully... oh dear, oh dear,' exclaimed the little man.

Fzzzzzzzzzzzzzzzzzzzzzz!

Louis watched the progress of the red cataball as it fizzed straight through a big thick tree branch and carried on towards the prisoners in the gaol wagon, who were eating their food behind the bars.

Fzzzzzzzzzzzzzzzzzz!

Louis noticed Mr Sand had closed his eyes as the ball went clean through the tin mug from which Mr Scurvy was drinking.

The liquid sloshed out of the holes in the mug and all over the Maggitts as Scurvy fell backwards off the upturned bucket that served as his seat.

Fzzzzzzzzzzzz!

The red cataball continued on out the other side of the cage towards a big rock, and fizzed right into it.

Louis couldn't see whether the cataball had gone through the other side of the rock; but there was certainly a lot of smoke coming from thc hole.

Wow! What a weapon, thought Louis, looking in awe at his new catapult.

'Oh dear, oh dear, oh dear,' Louis heard Mr Sand say again as they both ran towards the camp.

Ooops! worried Louis, I'm for it now.

'Ha, ha, ha.' Louis heard the soldiers roaring with laughter and saw them pointing at Scurvy and the Maggitts, and clutching their ribs.

After the laughter had subsided, one of the soldiers came up to him and bowed.

'Very good shot, Prince Louis. Excellent marksmanship.'

Louis glanced at Mr Sand for an indication of how to react.

'Yes, I agree,' said Gwithian Sand, with a smile and a wink.

'Thank you, Your Highness, for giving us a display of your prowess with the Kernow Catapult.'

With that, the King's Chief Surveyor & Mapmaker began clapping. All the soldiers clapped too.

Louis puffed himself up and strode around the camp looking very pleased with himself.

He would, however, have been very disturbed if he had heard what Mr Scurvy mumbled to the Maggitts as a trickle of blood ran down his chin.

'Prince or not, that boy will pay dearly for making me a laughing stock.

'Very dearly indeed!'

# TWENTY-NINE

## Plumper

Dribble panted along towards Washaway Wood as fast as his little legs would carry him. With his long tongue hanging down from the side of his jaw, and drool dripping on the road with every step, he held *Drym's Diary* between his tightly clenched teeth.

What the little hero didn't know was that the warm sticky liquid dripping constantly from his mouth had soaked into the diary and made it a bit soggy. Some of the pages had even become stuck together, and the ink was running.

Dribble was at the bottom of a big hill, and he could now see the little village of Washaway at the top, where Clevercloggs and the other gnomes lived.

As Dribble began the steep climb, he repeated one thought over and over. Clevercloggs will know what to do, Clevercloggs will know what to do, Clevercloggs will know…

Halfway up the hill, a very fat gnome waddled out from behind a tree, huffing and puffing as he panted along in his blue dungarees and red pointy hat, which almost matched the colour of his rosy cheeks.

The name 'Plumper' was stitched on the front of his dungarees. He was not much more than two feet tall and, like all male gnomes, he had been born with a bushy white beard, bushy white eyebrows, and a full head of curly white hair.

'Well what have we here? Are you lost little long dog?' asked the gnome, curling his thumbs around the braces of his dungarees as he leant back and stuck his very large tummy out.

Dribble shook his head in reply. This made his collar rattle. Plumper felt the collar between his short stumpy fingers for the source of the tinkling.

'*Dribble. Dust Dog. Property of M. Drym*,' he read aloud. 'So you're lost are you? Oh, and there's an address on here as well, would you like me to take you home?'

Dribble whined and whimpered and shook his head, trying to show Plumper that he definitely did *not* want to go home. He dropped the diary in front of the gnome, nudging it forwards with his nose.

Plumper picked up the diary and prized open a couple of pages that were not too badly stuck together. He screwed up his face a bit as he felt Dribble's sticky drool on the paper, but he was too polite to say anything about it.

'What strange words are these?' he mused, scratching his left bushy eyebrow. '*Jowbtjpo. Ebsloftt Ebz.* This isn't any language I know. I'm afraid I can't help you at all, Dribble.'

Dribble dropped his head in disappointment. He didn't know how to ask for Clevercloggs.

'Of course, Clevercloggs will know,' continued Plumper. 'He'll be back later on today and we've planned a surprise party for him. Come on, Dribble, we'll get you some water whilst we're waiting for Clevercloggs. We shan't be eating anything for now though, it's his five-hundredth birthday and we don't want to spoil the Grand Teafeast do we?'

Dribble's spirits lifted immediately. He *was* going to meet Clevercloggs to show him the diary after all.

Not only that, he had only ever had cold porridge to eat, and soon he would be going to his very first birthday feast.

An extra large gobbet of drool dripped from the corner

of his mouth as he thought of all the tasty food they would have at the party.

But the little dog would not have been so happy if he'd looked behind him towards the old oak tree at the bottom of the hill.

For there, perched on a gnarled old branch and still watching Dribble's every move with his beady eyes, was Craw, Wendron's carrier crow.

# THIRTY

## Eden Valley

A scowling Sheviok Scurvy gripped the bars of the cage tightly, still mumbling menacingly under his breath, as he watched Gwithian Sand lead Louis away from the laughing soldiers and the gaol wagon.

Teacher and pupil sat down under the same tree as before.

'Now you are dressed properly and know a little of the ways of Kernowland,' said Mr Sand very seriously, 'I must tell you more about the history of Erthwurld in general, and Eden Valley in particular.

'You will have to learn quickly and remember as much as you can. Everyone knows these stories and you must not be an exception.'

Louis paid as much attention as he could as Mr Sand began.

'Many centuries ago, an ancient sage called Trethurgy Timmits had an idea. He gathered together a group of people to help him with his plan.

'They collected plants from all over the planet and re-planted them here at Eden Valley, a huge garden complex formed in the hollow of a clay pit.

'They took the name from the story of the "Garden of Eden", which tells how a garden paradise was created at the beginning of time, for people to live in with no worries or problems.

'Sage Timmits and his friends wanted to create a garden paradise in Kernowland, just like the original Garden of Eden.

'But lots of the plants would not have been able to

live in the Kernowland climate, so they had to build the big domes.

'Yes, for plants from the jungles and deserts,' said Louis confidently.

'Quite correct,' continued Mr Sand, rather surprised that Louis knew this. 'It was lucky they did build the domes, because the ancient people of Erthwurld went on to destroy much of the natural habitat with scientific experiments that were not in the cause of Good and Right.

'Just like in the story of the Garden of Eden, the people didn't realise what they had been given, and they ruined it by behaving badly.

# THIRTY-ONE

# Dwarflings and Gigantics

'Experiments were carried out on the plants and animals – and later, even people. The aim was to change living beings by tampering with their cells. The scientists put plant cells into animals, animal cells into plants, and much more. These experiments changed the colours and shapes and sizes of all types of things. They called it "genetic mutation".

'Before long, a whole new type of science developed all over Erthwurld... "mutationeering". At first the mutationeers made some useful changes. They grew the ears of people on to mice and were able to use things like this for improving medicine. They cloned harmless animals like sheep to make a plentiful food supply. They made dolphins even cleverer than they already were, to help with rescues at sea.'

'I think I've heard of some things like that,' said Louis, as Mr Sand continued.

'But the people of the wurld did not know the dangerous game they were playing. Some thought that a good way to make money would be to give children living toys. So the mutationeers made Dwarflings – such as tiny ponies and miniature lions and tigers and gorillas – for children to play with.'

That sounds cool, thought Louis to himself; it must be great to have a living, breathing, moving toy.

But then Mr Sand told him something that made him change his mind.

'These tiny animals were condemned to terrible lives.

As soon as they were old enough, they were taken from their mothers, put to sleep, then boxed up and put on the shelves for sale. Living toys were in such demand that parents sometimes fought over them in the shops.'

'When they were given their new presents, the children woke them up by bathing them in a special solution that came in the box.

'But because they had been taught to think of them as toys rather than pets, the children did not care for these animals properly. They fed them on all the wrong things, like chocolate and ice-cream, and kept them in tiny cages in their bedrooms and sheds – and even made them fight each other for fun.

'And even worse, when the latest new Dwarfling was made available in the shops, the children simply threw away their old ones by releasing them in the fields or jungles or deserts near their homes. Thousands of discarded Dwarflings now roam the Erth, all struggling to survive because they were not designed for a life in the wild.'

Louis thought this was a horrible thing to happen to tiny animals. He didn't think he would want to throw away a Dwarfling if he were given one.

Mr Sand continued: 'Then the countries began to compete with each other, to see who could come up with bigger and better mutations. Mega-growth experiments were conducted. That's when the Gigantics appeared: giant plants, giant animals, and even giant people.

# THIRTY-TWO

## Chewing Creatures

'Then the leaders decided to make living, breathing war machines, and a whole new species of being was artificially evolved – the Chewing Creatures.'

'What are they?' asked a wide-eyed Louis.

'Colossal monsters, designed only to kill and feast on flesh, with a single purpose… to crush the enemy and then eat them as a reward.

'You cannot imagine a Chewing Creature until you have encountered one close up.

'They are unlike anything you have ever seen. Pictures cannot capture the full horror of the screeching and the stench.

'Some have huge claws or jaws or both. Others have four tusks, or five horns, or six sabre teeth. The Cyclops Chewing Creatures have only one eye, whilst others have twenty or more.

'Unfortunately, I fear we will certainly meet more than one of these massive monsters when we begin the rescue of your sister.

'For when we leave the safety of Kernowland's borders, we will become Chewing Creature prey in the hunting grounds of Erthwurld.'

# THIRTY-THREE

## The Science Wars

Louis tried *not* to imagine the Chewing Creatures, as Mr Sand continued.

'It wasn't long before each competing country cloned the mutated monsters, and vast armies of identical fighting beasts were spawned in the Chewing Creature factories of the wurld, all ready to make war at the bidding of their misguided masters.

'At the same time, the competing powers created terrible weapons of wurld destruction: weapons that could create havoc with the weather; weapons that could obliterate whole countries in a single second.

'The leaders and their war scientists even tested these weapons underground, beneath the surface of their own countries, creating harmful vibrations which began the ruination of the very land they were trying to defend.

'The Science Wars set nation against nation, continent against continent, as they all struggled for scientific supremacy over one another.

'For centuries, the weapons of wurld destruction used in these wars ravaged the planet.

'The weather and climates were changed all over Erthwurld. Volcanoes erupted everywhere, spewing out great lava flows that destroyed everything in their path. Whole mountains were flattened, whilst new ranges were created in their place. Rainforests withered, earthquakes shook whole continents, and huge waves flooded the cities and towns.

'In the north, the snow fell continuously for decades, creating the great snow plains we now call Snowland. Elsewhere, the rain pelted down in torrents, causing floods that left us with Lakeland and Riverland. In the east, the sun beat down mercilessly for centuries, leaving little but the vast, parched desert that today we call Sandland.

'All this created new lands and environments that Mother Nature never intended.

'Many of the original plant species were wiped out, along with nearly all the animals and most of the people.'

# THIRTY-FOUR

## Evile

Louis listened intently as Mr Sand told him more.

'In the altered Erthwurld that followed the genetic mutation experiments and the Science Wars, even more terrible mutations grew out of the ashes; the result of mating between the mutated species.

'The so-called "science masters" had long lost control of their Chewing Creatures, and the great hungry beasts were free to roam what was left of the Erth, crushing and eating everything in their path, including each other.

'It was "survival of the fittest" gone mad.'

Mr Sand saw that Louis looked genuinely horrified by what he was hearing, and tried to say something that might reassure his worried looking pupil.

'But we must never give up hope and faith, Prince Louis,' he said. 'And that is what we have here at Eden Valley, and in Kernowland: hope and faith that if we hold on to the right values and keep doing good science, we can put right the wrongs of the past and avoid making the same mistakes in the future.'

'But how, if everything has been ruined?' asked Louis.

'Well, fortunately,' answered Mr Sand with a hopeful smile, 'Eden Valley was untouched by the Science Wars, so many of the original plants that Mother Nature intended, were saved right here.

'Our dream is that one day we can restore Erthwurld to the way it was meant to be. We aim to use science in the cause of Right and Good.'

Louis nodded as he listened because he thought this sounded very sensible.

'When we go into the domes,' continued Mr Sand, 'you'll see lots of people wearing long green coats. They are the good scientists on whom we are pinning our hopes.

'Our leader, King Kernow, is a good man too, which is so important for the success of our plan to re-plant the wurld with good seeds. It is always very important to have leaders with vision and good hearts.'

'Have you started putting the natural plants back around the world?' asked Louis.

'Oh my, if only it were that simple,' sighed Mr Sand. 'Alas that is not as easy as it might seem.

'For out of the chaos of the Science Wars rose a dictator, the like of whom the wurld had never seen.

'He was evil incarnate... and he called himself Evile.

'No one knows from whence he came nor how he acquired his awesome dark powers. He simply appeared and declared for all to hear that his plan was to conquer every land in Erthwurld and bring them under the yoke of his Evil Empire.

'Every morning and every night, Evile drank one drop of an elixir that kept him young and strong. Throughout the passing centuries, legions of his armies lived and died for him, whilst he gained no more than a few years in age.

'Evile crushed all resistance to become the Supreme Emperor, bringing darkness, slavery, fear, and death in his wake wherever he went. He now reigns over every land of Erthwurld... with one exception.'

'Kernowland!' exclaimed Louis triumphantly.

'Yes, Kernowland. The last place on Erth where the Light of Goodness still shines.

'This wonderful Kingdom was untouched throughout

the troubles that plagued the rest of the wurld, because Godolphin the Great had discovered the secret of White Light Magic just in time. And it was the power of The One Light that protected Kernowland from the dark forces of Evile's Empire.

'We'll be at Kernow Castle for the next White Light Ceremony, so you'll be able to see it.'

'When is it?' asked Louis in eager anticipation.

'In two days' time,' answered Mr Sand.

'On midsummer's morning.'

# THIRTY-FIVE

## Gurt and Lasher

Tizzie came round from her faint to find that her hands were tied at the front so that her arms were stretched and she was hugging a big thick mast.

She strained her neck around to see what was behind her. All the children were still in their lines. Jack was looking very worriedly at her.

'Now, slavelings, this is what you'll get if you don't behave,' growled Pigleg. 'Nothing like a taste of Lasher to bring some order and quiet to a ship.'

Errrhhh!

A door creaked.

The sound came from in front of Tizzie, and she strained her neck forward around the mast, to see Purgy come out, the tattoo-mouth grinning wildly.

Then came Gurt.

The punisher was so tall that he had to bend double to get through the doorway. Standing to his full height, he cast a long, wide shadow on the deck. He stretched and yawned loudly, as if he'd been awoken from a deep sleep.

Tizzie could see right into Gurt's mouth. He had no tongue.

Then she noticed the black whip in his right hand. It was wound in two loops and had a long, black, wooden handle.

Lasher.

Tizzie started to panic. She didn't want to be whipped. She pulled and wriggled and tried desperately to free her arms, but the bonds were too tight.

Gurt's bulging eyes glared around him, as if he was looking for someone to blame for waking him up. He looked first at the lines of children, and then at Tizzie. She pulled even more frantically at the ropes around her wrists.

Glaring once more at all the children, Gurt raised Lasher's handle above his head.

'Gurrhhhh,' he gurgled, as he brought the whip's handle quickly down towards the deck.

Thwcrack!

All the children jumped and took a pace backwards.

Except Jack, who stood with his arms folded, scowling at Gurt in defiance.

Tizzie struggled even harder to free herself.

'Gurrhhhh,' gurgled Gurt again as he pounded forward, the deck creaking under the weight of his every step. Creak followed creak until the punisher stopped about ten paces behind Tizzie.

'Six lashes, Gurt,' instructed Pigleg. 'And make 'em gooduns. We need some discipline aboard this vessel afore we set sail.'

Tizzie strained her neck to look behind her once more. Out of the corner of her eye, she could just see Gurt raising Lasher's long handle above his head.

She closed her eyes and tensed every muscle in her body, getting ready for the first cut of the lash.

# THIRTY-SIX

## The Carnivore Cage

When Mr Sand had finished telling Louis the history of Eden Valley and Erthwurld, they went inside to eat.

Food was being served in the connecting building between the two big white domes. A long banner above the entrance read: *Indigo Eating Place*.

A number of separate food counters were arranged in a row, each with a sign above it. Mr Sand walked straight over to one with a sign that read: *Mrs Portwrinkle's Pastys, Pastries & Pies*.

He bought two of Mrs Portwrinkle's pastys, one for himself and one for Louis.

'Mrs Portwrinkle is Chief Cook to the King at Kernow Castle,' explained Mr Sand as they sat down on a bench at a table.

'She makes the best pastys in the wurld, and everyone in Kernowland eats them whenever they can. Most people have one every day, sometimes two or even three!

'I have it on good authority that Mrs Portwrinkle, a rather large lady by any standards, eats a pasty side-order with every single meal.'

Louis didn't know whether to admit it, but he had never had a pasty before. He looked at the food. It was made of shortcrust pastry and shaped a bit like a small, flat rugby ball. Piping hot, it smelt fantastic.

Louis bit into the pasty and tasted the juicy meat and potatoes and onions inside. He decided immediately that Mr Sand was right; Mrs Portwrinkle's pastys were absolutely delicious!

When no one was looking, Louis popped some of the lovely pasty inside his top pocket for Misty.

'*Thank you, my friend*,' said the squeaky little voice in his head.

After lunch, Mr Sand said: 'We've still got some time. Would you like to look around the Jungle Dome?'

'Yes please, Mr Sand,' said Louis, leaping off the bench and walking quickly towards the Jungle Dome entrance. Mr Sand waddled as fast as he could to catch up, and they went in.

On entering, Louis immediately noticed the wet and humid atmosphere of a rainforest, and heard the unmistakcable sound of cascading water. A roaring waterfall plunged from the top of the dome and ran down the sloping landscape into a pool at the bottom, creating a misty haze around the pool.

Mud paths weaved around the slope, allowing Louis and his teacher to walk freely between the plants.

As they made their way along the narrow pathways, Mr Sand told Louis about all the plants that had been preserved from the time before the mutation experiments and the Science Wars.

After a while, Louis noticed a disturbing sign pointing ahead: *Carnivore Cage*.

'What's that, Mr Sand?' he asked tentatively, recognising the word 'carnivore' and remembering vividly what Tizzie had said in the car about meat-eating plants.

'Well,' answered Mr Sand, 'originally there were all sorts of carnivorous plants that Mother Nature designed to eat meat. They fed on small insects, trapping their prey before dissolving and digesting it in their special juices.

'But the mutationeers created some real monster carnivores with their plant and animal growth experiments;

creatures so dangerous they have to be tied down and caged if there are people around.

'We have one of these mutant meat-eating plant-creatures in the Carnivore Cage. Our Erth scientists are trying to see where the mutationeers went wrong, so we can try to put it right and restore the wurld to the way Mother Nature intended. Follow me, I'll show you.'

Louis wasn't at all sure he wanted to see a giant meat-eating plant-creature that had to be tied down and caged, but he followed because he felt safe when Mr Sand was with him.

As they rounded a corner on the path, they passed beneath a warning sign written in large red letters:

# DANGER!
## KEEP OUT – CARNIVORE CAGE AHEAD.
## AUTHORISED PERSONS ONLY
## BEYOND THIS POINT.

# THIRTY-SEVEN

## Brazilian Brainboilers

Louis gulped as they walked straight on for a few paces, then down some steep steps. At the bottom, he froze, staring in awe at the sight before his eyes.

There, behind the bars of a metal cage about the size of a house, was a dark purple tree with a thick trunk. All its branches were tied down with strong ropes, secured by pegs hammered into the ground.

Two men in green coats were scraping some material from a branch. The tree winced and pulled at the restraining ropes as if the scraping hurt.

Louis instinctively moved forward, to ask the men to stop hurting the tree.

'Don't get any closer to the cage, Louis,' warned Mr Sand, grabbing his pupil by the shoulder.

'Is it dangerous then?' asked Louis, fearing the answer he already knew.

'Very. We've only got this one adult of the species at the moment. It's the most dangerous tree-creature in the wurld.'

'What's it called?' asked Louis, his eyes opening wider by the second.

'The species is the "Brazilian Brainboiler",' answered Mr Sand. 'The original brainboilers were created by the mutationeers in a country called Brazil, a land much changed by the Science Wars.'

'Why is it called a brainboiler?' asked Louis, not entirely sure that he wanted to know.

'The mutationeers thought it would be clever to make

a plant which would eat the part of animals that the people didn't want. So, they designed a tree-creature that would only want to eat brains.

'The original brainboiler design was a hollow trunk, which created a well for boiling digestive juices that served as a cooking cauldron.

'People threw the brains of dead animals in to the cauldron, and the plant-creatures boiled and melted them for food. The original brainboilers were little more than brain-eating dustbins.'

Louis stared at the tree-creature with renewed terror, as his tutor continued the lesson.

'Then the mutationeers bred a variation of the brainboilers to protect the properties of rich people.

'They took the cells of ferocious guard-dogs and baboons and vultures, mixed them all up, and put them in to the brainboilers. They also gave the new brainboilers a brain of their own. These ferocious, thinking brainboilers were the result, and they were sold as guard-trees.'

'How can they be guard-trees?' asked Louis, now even more worried. 'They can't chase anyone, can they?'

'No, brainboilers can't move across the ground,' answered Mr Sand, 'but they have twelve long branch-arms, each of which tapers down to a long flexible vine at the end. They were designed to be used as whips to see off trespassers and burglars.

'As you can see, we've had to secure this brainboiler's branch-arms with ropes and pegs, but normally the branch-arms are held high whilst the vines dangle down so that their tips just touch the ground in readiness for use against intruders.'

'How do they know where the burglars are?' asked Louis.

'They were also bred with twelve staring eyes, each positioned just underneath the trunk end of one of their branch-arms. When their branch-arms are raised, they can see in every direction at once.

'The eyes never blink, in case they should miss something. Look, if you come to the side here, you can see one of the staring eyes under that branch-arm.'

Louis looked, taking care not to go any closer to the bars of the cage than he needed to. It was hard to see because, as Mr Sand said, all the branch-arms were tied down and the eyes were obscured beneath them.

But, in one branch-armpit, he could just make out an unblinking, staring, orange eye.

A small cloud of steam hissed as it rose into the air from behind the eyeball.

'The steam keeps the eyeball moist,' informed Mr Sand.

Louis stared at the steam hissing from the brainboiler's eyeball as Mr Sand continued.

'If you walked around any of these tree-creatures, it would be at least twelve paces. This one is a real monster, the biggest of the species, a male more than twenty paces around.

'He's called Monstro.'

# THIRTY-EIGHT

## Octogon

Tizzie said a silent prayer, asking for the lash not to hurt too much. She squeezed the mast tightly, trembling in fear of the first stroke.

Suddenly, there was a shout from high above.

'Cap'n, it's Octogon on the starboard bow!'

Tizzie looked up.

The shout was from the pirate on lookout duty in the crow's nest at the top of the mast. He was pointing out to sea.

'Well spotted, Eagle Eye,' shouted Pigleg, as he pulled a little telescope from his inside pocket and put it to his good eye.

Tizzie looked. All the children looked. Gurt, Cudgel, Purgy, and all the other pirates looked.

Tizzie could see the fear in everyone's eyes. Except Pigleg, who didn't seem scared at all.

'Make ready for giant octoplus attack,' barked the Captain.

All the pirates ran to take up their positions. Some ran below to man the guns.

Pigleg's face was now next to Tizzie's ear.

'I'll attend to you later, Little Miss Troublemouth,' he snarled. 'But for now I've got a large orange octoplus with eighty-eight legs to deal with.'

Click, thud. Click, thud. Click, thud. Click, thud.

Tizzie watched Captain Pigleg race-hop over to the starboard side of the ship.

'Bring it on, rubber legs,' she heard him shout as he

shook his gold hook in the air at the huge wave that was fast approaching and growing by the second.

Now Jack was untying the ropes that bound her.

'Thanks,' she sighed with relief.

'Quick, up to the top, there's no time to lose,' he urged, as he began climbing the tall mast, motioning for her to follow him.

Tizzie had only got a few feet up the mast before she saw the moving mountain of water heading straight for the ship.

Looming ever closer inside the wave was what looked like a massive orange ball with lots of orange snakes attached to it, all wriggling and writhing and squirming in every direction.

As the huge orange ball in the wave got within a few yards of the ship, eight blazing red eyes and a giant beak opened on the front of it.

Tizzie was petrified. She couldn't move a muscle as she heard Pigleg shout above the noise of the wave.

'Brace yerselves, mates.'

Cacrash!

The huge orange ball hit the ship with the force of a fifty-ton rhinoceros. *The Revenger* lurched horribly, first towards the wave and then back the other way.

'Aaaaaarrrrrgggghhhhhhhhhhhh!'

Eagle Eye, the lookout at the top of the mast, screamed a very long scream as he fell over one hundred feet, straight into the open beak of the octoplus.

A mass of orange tentacles swarmed over the deck, sweeping up children and pirates alike, and waving them about in the air.

'Quickly, quickly,' shouted Jack, 'we must get up to the top of the mast.'

This brought Tizzie to her senses. She started climbing

up the mast once more.

Just then, a long orange tentacle grabbed around the mast and Tizzie's waist at the same time, squeezing the breath out of her.

'Help me!' she screamed in terror.

Thwcrack.

Down on the deck, Gurt was aiming Lasher at the tentacle squeezing Tizzie. He scored a hit first time, and a deep cut opened up in the long rubbery arm, which recoiled back overboard immediately, leaving a trail of pale blue blood on the deck.

Tizzie looked down at Gurt.

'Gurrhhh,' he gurgled, beating his chest and raising Lasher in readiness for another strike at one of the many orange tentacles now engulfing the ship.

Tizzie continued climbing. Halfway to the top, she glanced down again.

Octogon had a hold on nearly everybody. The children were all screaming as they were waved wildly about. All the pirates were cursing.

A tentacle encircled Pigleg. His arms were free and he hacked away at the tentacle with his hook and his cutlass. Mr Cudgel was bashing another tentacle with his truncheon arm.

Thwcrack. Thwcrack.

Gurt still had his feet on the deck, and he was thrashing around in every direction with Lasher. Pale blue blood spurted and squirted everywhere.

Boom!... Boom!

The sound of cannon fire startled Tizzie.

Over the side of the ship, she watched as Octogon absorbed two shots at close range. This blasted the great orange beast away from the ship a small distance, and

Tizzie thought it must surely be wounded.

But to her disappointment, within a few moments, the monster seemed to have recovered.

Tentacles swarmed everywhere once more, grabbing up children and pirates, and waving them about as they screamed and shouted and gasped for breath.

'Cannon and cutlass are no good against a chewing creature that size,' she heard Jack say as they reached the crow's nest at the top of the mast.

'What can stop it then?' murmured Tizzie. 'Are we all going to die?'

'Shooosh, I'm concentrating,' scolded Jack.

Tizzie watched as Jack stood up straight, put his head back, looked to the skies, opened out his arms, closed his eyes… and sang in a way Tizzie had never heard anyone sing before.

'AaaaaaaOoooooooEeeeeeeAaaaaaa.'

Tizzie looked down. Almost immediately, Octogon, the giant orange octoplus, stopped its wriggling and writhing and squirming, and dropped all the children and pirates it was holding.

Some fell back onto the deck with a crunch; others fell into the water with a splash.

'AaaaaaaOoooooooEeeeeeeAaaaaaa.'

Now Tizzie saw Octogon shaking uncontrollably, creating lots of splashing waves that rocked the ship from side to side.

After a few more moments of Jack's song, the monster simply closed its eyes and began to sink quietly back into the depths.

'AaaaaaaOoooooooEeeeeeeAaaaaaa.'

Jack continued his song until the huge, fearsome beast had completely disappeared under the water from whence it came.

Now all eyes were looking up at the crow's nest, towards the source of the strange but beautiful sound... Jack.

'We'll done, lad,' shouted Pigleg, after he had picked himself up from the deck below.

'How did you do that?' quizzed Tizzie.

'If I tell you a secret, do you promise not to tell it to anyone?'

'I swear,' swore Tizzie.

'I'm an apprentice Wizard. That was a Sendaway Spell I was singing. The Red Wizard, Reddadom himself, was teaching me the ways of Red Magic before I was kidnapped by Cudgel and Purgy, after I was tricked into drinking a sleeping potion.

'Pigleg mustn't find out I'm Reddadom's apprentice, or he'll try to get me to use Red Magic to help him do bad things. He might threaten to hurt the other children and hold them hostage to make me do it; and then what could I do?

'We'd better get down below now. I'll tell you more later.'

'Okay,' agreed Tizzie, now even more impressed with her new mysterious, brave, and clever friend.

By the time they had climbed back down to the bottom of the mast, all the children and pirates in the water were clambering back on to the ship, using ropes and ladders that the others had put over the side.

'Any casualties, Mr Cudgel?' enquired Pigleg.

'We lost Eagle Eye; poor blighter didn't stand a chance. Went in whole, straight down the beast's gullet.'

The first mate then patted Jack on the back as he continued. 'Apart from that, looks like it's just a few cuts and bruises all round thanks to this young lad.'

'Aye,' agreed Pigleg, looking down at Jack.

'Now lad, Pirate's Code says we've got to give ye a

reward to match the deed, lest Lady Luck sees fit to send us to the bottom of the sea before our time.

'Now, I'm not a superstitious fellow meself, see, but me crewmates are to a man, isn't that right, mates?'

'Aye aye, Cap'n,' cheered the pirates in unison, except Gurt, who was leaning against the cabin house, sleeping, and snoring loudly.

'That's decided then. So what'll it be, young feller? A piece of treasure from Pigleg's own chest? A job with us as an apprentice pirate? Even entitled to 'is freedom one day if he takes that option I s'pose, eh mates?'

'Aye aye, Cap'n,' cheered the pirates in unison again.

All eyes were on Jack. He thought for a moment.

'I don't want anything for myself, sir. But I'd like you to spare the girl her lashes.'

The ship went silent.

The pirates looked around at each other in utter disbelief. A murmuring began, which got louder and louder, and then louder still.

'Quiet mates,' barked Pigleg, holding up his hook to silence the crew once more.

'Hmmm, I see. Like that, is it?'

The pirate captain looked at Tizzie, and then looked back at Jack, scratching his chin with his hook as if thinking hard.

'So be it. The girl gets no lashes. Debt repaid under the Pirate's Code. All agreed, lads?'

'Aye aye, Cap'n,' mumbled the pirates, although a lot less enthusiastically than before. They seemed a little confused by Jack's decision, and very disappointed that there would be no lashing today.

With his crew's superstitions satisfied, Pigleg obviously wanted to move things on.

'Now, get these slaves down below, quick as you please. They've got an appointment with a hungry red pig to get to... and we're standing here wastin' the wind.'

Tizzie looked at Jack, and he smiled back kindly.

A little tear trickled down her face as she and all the other children were herded back into the hold. But it wasn't sadness she felt, it was altogether something different.

'Cast off and set sail for Jungleland, if you will, Mr Cudgel.'

Pigleg shouted his orders just as the hatch was thrown down.

Crash!

As Tizzie sat huddled with all the other children for warmth in the dark, cold hold, she found herself trembling simply at the thought of what Red Grunter might do to her and the other children.

Two words churned over and over in her mind.

Boar bait... Boar bait... BOAR BAIT!

# THIRTY-NINE

## Monstro

As Louis stared at Monstro, the Brazilian brainboiler, Mr Sand told him more about the tree-creature.

'At the bottom of his cauldron, deep inside his trunk, sits a mutant brain that can withstand the boiling temperatures of his digestive juices.

'These guard-trees with brains were in great demand at first. Very rich people kept whole packs of them to protect their mansion houses and vast lands.

'But the mutationeers did not know the trouble it would cause, giving the brainboilers their own brain. The more the tree-creatures boiled and absorbed the animal brains they were fed, the cleverer they got.

'One day, Monstro used one of his vines as a lasso to grab a burglar by the ankle instead of whipping at him to make him go away.

'Then the brainboiler whisked the burglar into the air, hung him upside down, and slowly lowered his head into the cauldron of digestive juices, gradually boiling the man's brain inside his own skull until it melted and ran from his nose and ears and eye sockets.

'Urgghhhhh!' exclaimed Louis, horrified and revolted at what he was hearing.

'Then Monstro threw away the body and waited for his next victim,' continued Mr Sand.

'Before long, all the brainboilers followed Monstro's example and were taking their own live prey. Once they had tasted warm, living brains, they wanted nothing else.

'From that day on, the owners did not dare to go near their own guard-trees.

'The brainboilers began to breed in the wild, and the jungle became infested with them. Most people would no longer even approach the jungle perimeter, let alone cross over it.

'Through the centuries, these intelligent creatures have become highly efficient predators, with one driving desire... to feed on live, warm brains.

'In the wild, they would mostly take the brains of small animals like monkeys and birds, but this one would certainly like to boil our brains; he hasn't had warm, live food since we brought him here.'

Mr Sand noticed Louis had gone white with fear.

'Now, I think that's probably enough about brainboilers for one day,' he said, beckoning Louis to follow him as they climbed back up the steps and away from the Carnivore Cage.

When they were some way down the path, Mr Sand patted Louis on the shoulder and said: 'I'll leave you looking around for a while. I have to discuss one or two things about the prisoners with Lieutenant Liskeard.

'As I said before, the people with long green coats are the Erth scientists. You can ask them as many questions as you like. They'll be happy to help anyone wearing that royal uniform. Remember, if anyone asks, you're a cousin of the King.'

'Thank you for everything, Mr Sand,' said Louis, who was looking forward to seeing some more of the jungle plants in the dome.

Mr Sand smiled warmly as he began walking away.

Then he suddenly turned back and spoke to Louis in a low warning voice.

'Whatever you do, Louis, don't go too near the Carnivore Cage. Monstro is an extremely sly, vicious, and dangerous tree-creature. Please make sure you stay behind the barriers out of reach of his branch-arms and lasso vines.

'Even from inside the cage, Monstro is capable of killing people with one swipe through the bars. He'd kill out of pure spite.'

Louis nodded in agreement. It sounded like very good advice.

After Mr Sand had gone, Louis went off up the path and looked at more of the weird and wonderful plants in the Jungle Dome.

But, after a while, he couldn't resist the opportunity to take just one last look at Monstro.

Sensibly, he thought he'd do it from a safe distance. He stood on one of the higher paths, and lent over the fence so that he could look down on the cage.

From above, Louis could see the digestive juices boiling in the cooking cauldron.

The liquid was cloudy but he could just make out Monstro's veiny purple brain submerged at the bottom of the cauldron. The brain was about the size of a football. It was pulsating in and out, creating small ripples on the surface of the boiling juices.

Louis heard a faint snoring. He looked in his pocket and smiled to see that Misty was sound asleep. He thought his little friend was probably full after his pasty.

As Louis lent against the fence, the Kaski dug into his hip a little, reminding him that it was there. He remembered that he hadn't tested all the blades yet.

Louis took out his survival knife and began opening all the blades and other tools, like scissors and screwdrivers, from their slots and housings.

When he had opened them all, he held up the Kaski in front of his face.

Wow, he thought, there are loads of them. He was really pleased with his new knife.

Then Louis started putting all the blades and tools away, snapping them back into their slots and pushing them into their housings. But on snapping shut the last sharp blade, he cut his finger.

'Ouch,' he cried, as he felt the pinch.

It was only a little cut, but Louis was so startled that he dropped the knife. It went over the fence, bounced on a rock on the slope and fell straight down into the Carnivore Cage.

He looked down.

The knife had landed about one pace from Monstro's trunk.

Louis didn't know what to do. Misty was asleep. Mr Sand was nowhere to be seen.

Then he saw that the two scientists in green coats had gone from the cage and left the door slightly ajar.

Louis really wanted his knife back, and wondered if he should try to get it himself.

He was absolutely terrified at that prospect but, since Monstro was securely tied down, he thought it would probably be all right to go in to the cage for a few seconds.

After all, the scientists had been in there for ages earlier. And if he was really, really quick, no one would even notice.

Louis walked briskly along the winding path and down the steep steps until he reached the Carnivore Cage.

He approached the cage carefully, and was so scared that his legs began to shake.

As Louis moved closer to the cage, the brainboiler stirred a little, as if it could sense the boy's presence.

Opening the door just enough to enter, Louis crept into the cage. His heart began to pound, and his palms began to sweat.

Then he heard a pitiful whimpering in his head.

'*Ueww. Uewww. Uewwwwwwww.*'

It sounded like a wounded puppy.

Louis' expression must have shown the clever tree-creature that he had heard the whimpering.

'*Leetell ma-an, leetell ma-an, won't you help me, por favor?*' whined a Brazilian voice in his head. '*They 'ave tied me up. I don't want to 'urt anyone. I just want to go 'ome. Untie my arms, por favor, so I can 'ave a leetell stretch.*'

Louis knew it was Monstro speaking to him, and he began to feel a bit sorry for the tree-creature who was all tied up and being scraped and tested. After all, Monstro had a brain, so surely he must have feelings too.

But then Louis remembered Mr Sand's words of warning, and common sense prevailed.

Trying not to listen to Monstro's pleading inside his head, Louis crept towards his Kaski, watching warily for any sign of sudden movement from the tree-creature.

'*Ruff! Ruff!*' barked Monstro as he strained at the ropes pinning his branch arms to the ground.

Louis was startled, and froze on the spot, his heart pounding even harder inside his chest.

'Phew.'

He sighed with relief to see that Monstro was still securely restrained. Plucking up his courage again, Louis moved closer to the trunk, where his Kaski lay waiting for recovery.

As he got within two paces, he noticed the trunk was

covered in something like shiny moss. Then he realised what it was.

Monstro had fur!

Bending down to pick up the knife, Louis looked up under a branch-arm into the pit where it met the trunk.

A steaming orange eye glared down at him as his fingers fumbled about on the ground and curled around the knife.

'*I AM MONSTRO!*' declared the brainboiler, as twelve huge puffs of steam hissed from behind each of his eyeballs.

'*I weel boil your brain and take my time about eeet!*'

Knife in shaking hand, Louis began backing away in a stoop, warily watching the brainboiler all the while.

'*RUUUFF!*' barked Monstro again, so loudly that Louis nearly jumped out of his skin. He stepped backwards so quickly that he tripped over one of the restraining ropes.

Lying on the ground, trembling, Louis noticed his fall had loosened the pinning peg securing the rope. He got up as fast as he could and took a pace towards the peg, grabbing up a stone with which to bang it back into the ground.

But he was too late.

'*Grrrrrrrrrrrowwwlll!*'

Monstro growled ferociously as he tugged with all his might at the rope, tearing the pinning peg from the ground. Louis was rooted to the spot with fear as the peg flew through the air towards him and whizzed past his left ear.

Before he could duck, the rope swung upwards and struck him on the cheek, knocking him to the ground again and making him drop his knife.

Terrified, Louis quickly jumped to his feet, turned about, and ran for his life towards the cage door.

Just as he got there and grasped the handle, he felt a

vine wrap around his ankle.

'*Not so fast, leetell warm-brain,*' said the voice in his head.

With that, Louis felt the tug of the vine on his leg. He gripped the handle of the cage door as tightly as he could with both hands.

The tree-creature tugged.

Louis gripped tighter.

Monstro tugged harder.

Louis was no match for the tree-creature's strength. He felt the skin of his fingers tear as his hands were ripped from the handle.

Now he was being dragged along the ground on his belly. He dug his fingers into the mud, trying desperately to save himself. But the dragging just got faster and faster until he felt one hard tug on his ankle, and he was flying up into the air.

'*Ha-hahaaaa!*' mocked Monstro, as Louis found himself dangling upside-down with his cape falling over his head towards the ground.

A familiar squeaky voice spoke inside his head.

'*Help! I can't hold on much longer.*' It was Misty.

Louis moved his chin towards his chest to see Misty hanging on to the top of the shirt pocket by the claws of his two back paws, the golden key gripped securely between his teeth.

'*Two lovely warm brains, all for me, for me,*' gloated Monstro hungrily, as he slowly lowered his prey down towards the cauldron of digestive juices that served as his belly.

Louis felt a tiny tug on his pocket. Glancing at Misty again, he saw that his little friend was now hanging on with only one paw gripping the top of the pocket, the key still between his teeth.

'*I'm losing my grip. I'm going to fall in,*' squeaked the terrified little mouse.

Louis looked erthward.

The frothing liquid loomed ever closer as Monstro eased them down and down towards the cooking cauldron.

Louis felt the scalding heat of the steam on his face.

The ravenous voice in his head was triumphant.

'*Two leetell warm brains... ALL FOR MONSTRO!*'

# FORTY

## Drym's Fury

Melanchol Drym was shivering in his sleep. The afternoon had brought with it a cold breeze, which was blowing in through the open door.

Drym opened one of his piercing, deep-set, beady, black eyes, and looked around the room. Then he opened the other eye and looked out of the back window towards the rubbish heap.

Something's wrong, he thought.

He cocked his head to the left, and put his right ear slightly forward to listen out for any clues.

A twisted frown came over his face as he raised his long, pointy, grey nose in the air and sniffed.

Snnff! Snnff!

Drym's suspicions were confirmed by his highly-honed senses.

He couldn't see Dribble.

He couldn't hear Dribble.

And he couldn't smell Dribble.

'Dribble,' he murmured menacingly under his breath. This was normally enough to make the little dog come running up to the back door, whimpering submissively.

Nothing.

'DRIBBLE,' he shouted.

Silence.

It was at this moment that Drym spied the open drawer and the tell-tale trail of drool leading to the open front door.

'D-R-I-B-B-L-E!' he screamed, jumping out of the

chair and grabbing up Spikey all in the same movement.

Drym was furious, livid, incensed. He began kicking chairs and bashing Spikey down on the table.

Pots and pans, papers and cushions, everything flew all over the room as the bony grey man vented his rage.

Then his anger was replaced by fear. A sick feeling began to take hold in his belly.

'The diary, Spikey,' he mumbled under his breath. 'It's got everything in it. Details of where all the Kernowkids live, and their secrets, and our plans to kidnap them and put them in the dripping dungeon and sell them as slaves to the pirates.

'The Darkness Day invasion plans.

'The plotters and traitors.

'The other stuff that we wouldn't want anyone to know about.

'What's Wendron going to say?

'She'll put an itching spell on us at the very least.

'And the Young Master will lock us up in Thunder Tower and throw away the key.

'We may even be separated.'

Spikey didn't answer.

Drym continued ranting; his mood turning from fear to rage once more.

'That dog is trying to destroy our dream before it's even started, and after all we've done for him too, the ungrateful little stump-legged hound.

'Well, we're not going to let him do it. Oh no we're not!

'We're going to get that diary back, and decapitate and obliterate and annihilate that droopy-eared drooling mutt. Oh yes we are!'

Drym put Spikey's rusty iron point in a tapered hole in the stone wall of the house. The hole had the words

'Hurting' above it, and 'Hole' below it.

The growling grey man mumbled malevolent thoughts to himself as he twisted the stick around in the hole, first one way, and then the other.

'We'll makc you nice and sharp, Spikey. Oh, yes we will!

'There's going to be one less dust dog in Kernowland when we catch up with him. Oh yes there is!'

When he had finished sharpening Spikey in the 'Hurting Hole', Drym stuck its point in a cushion and swiped the stick from side to side.

The cushion flew off through the air, surrounding Drym in a cloud of feathers as he made his way towards the open door.

'That double-crossing Dachshund,' he fumed, slashing Spikey through the feathers in his rage.

'I'm going to kill that dog if it's the last thing I ever do.

'OH... YES... I... AM!'

# – NEXT –

After reading, *The Crystal Pool,* the first book in the *Kernowland* series, you may want certain questions answered:

Will Louis & Misty have their brains boiled by Monstro?

Will Tizzie get eaten bit by bit by Big Red Grunter?

Will Dribble be killed by Drym and Spikey?

What hideous creations will the mutationeers come up with next in Erthwurld?

Will Evile, the Supreme Emperor of Erthwurld, ever have the power to overcome Kernowland?

Many other questions may have been raised in your mind.

If so, you may get some answers by reading Book 2, the next title in the exciting Kernowland series:

### *Kernowland 2 Darkness Day*

Visit our websites for up-to-date information about new titles, publication dates, and popular school visits by the author

www.kernowland.com
www.erthwurld.com

# Kernowland

## An adventure in Erthwurld

See the following pages for illustrations of scenes and characters from the *Kernowland in Erthwurld* series...

as well as information about Jack Trelawny's new series, *13 Things*... and his **FREE school author visits**...

For colour illustrations from the *Kernowland in Erthwurld* series and more about the author, his books, and free school visits, see:

**www.jacktrelawny.com**

# Through the Crystal Pool

# Sold at the Polperro Inn

**www.jacktrelawny.com**

# Tizzie on the slave ship

# Monstro grabs Louis

# Sandland Spiderscorpion

# Invasion of Evil

**www.jacktrelawny.com**

# Clevercloggs the Explorer

# The Skycycle

**www.jacktrelawny.com**

# Ocotogon attacks!

# Eight upsified gnomes

www.jacktrelawny.com

# Danglefang hunts children

# The Guillotine of Sirap

**www.jacktrelawny.com**

# Questers in Jungleland

# Ratphael's rattweilers

**www.jacktrelawny.com**

# Big Red Grunter

# Questers at Uluru Rock

**www.jacktrelawny.com**

# Questers at Tipi City

# Colosseum of Dread

**www.jacktrelawny.com**

# The Nine Gnomes of Washaway Wood

Swinger

Flowerpot

Seesaw

Greenfingers

Clevercloggs

Fishalot

Plumper

Prickle

Longlegs

For colour illustrations from the *Kernowland in Erthwurld* series and more about the author, his books, and free school visits, see:

## www.jacktrelawny.com

# Jack Trelawny
## School Author - 'Edutainer'

Jack Trelawny first became known as a school author when he wrote six books in the *Kernowland in Erthwurld* series and began visiting schools.

Jack's second series, *13 Things*, is inspired by thirteen objects from the joint BBC and British Museum radio podcast project: *A History of the World in 100 Objects*.

# 100 Objects

When the BBC and British Museum had completed their joint project, they specially chose thirteen of the objects for children.

# 13 Objects = *13 Things*

As a children's author and regular school visitor, Jack Trelawny is discovering the true stories of these thirteen objects, and using each of them as inspiration for his historical fiction adventures in the new *13 Things* series.

## *13 Things* (1)

*The Emperor's Rhinoceros*, the first book in the *13 Things* series, was inspired by Dürer's Rhinoceros, Object 75 in the joint BBC / British Museum project.

## Dürer's Rhinoceros

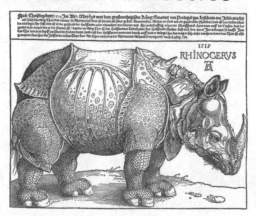

# Holt Farm Junior School at the British Museum after Jack Trelawny's author visit

The BBC and British Museum have provided websites, museum tours, and other free resources for each of the thirteen objects.

**Holt Farm Junior School at the British Museum**
**Photography by pupil, Leon T.**

Children enjoy using these resources to discover more about the *13 Things* after being introduced to them by Jack's stories.

See the following pages for more about the BBC and British Museum resources for children.

# BBC Primary History: World History Resources

The BBC children's website can be used as a free resource by teachers and parents for all thirteen of the objects in Jack Trelawny's *13 Things* series.

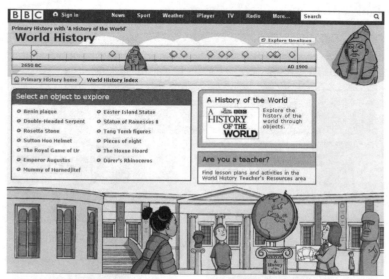

**BBC Primary History World History website**

---

### 13 Objects = *13 Things*

- Benin Plaque
- Double-Headed Serpent
- Rosetta Stone
- Sutton Hoo Helmet
- The Royal Game of Ur
- Emperor Augustus
- Mummy of Hornedjitef

- Easter Island Statue
- Statue of Ramesses II
- Tang Tomb Figures
- Pieces of Eight
- The Hoxne Hoard
- Dürer's Rhinoceros

---

There are quizzes, lesson plans, and activities on the site. For these and more children's resources at the BBC, see:

**www.bbc.co.uk/schools/primaryhistory/worldhistory**

# British Musuem:
# Learn World History
# with Objects or 'Things'

The British Museum has provided a website and offers free activity trails. These resources can be used by teachers and parents for all thirteen of the objects in Jack Trelawny's *13 Things* series.

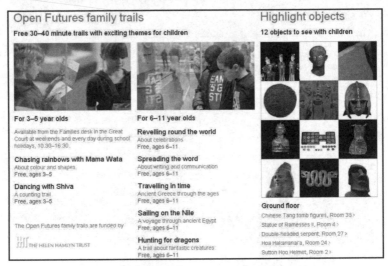

**British Museum website**

NOTE: Sometimes the Dürer's Rhinoceros woodcut object is not included in the relevant activity trail as it is preserved in storage. This means there may only be 12 of the 13 things/objects to view in the children's activity trail.

For these and more children's resources at the British Museum, see:

**www.britishmuseum.org/visiting/family_visits/ 13_objects_for_children.aspx**

**www.britishmuseum.org/visiting/family_visits/ activity_trails.aspx**

## *A History of the World in 100 Objects*

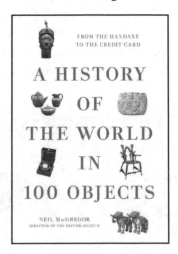

For adults interested in all 100 objects, there is a wonderful illustrated book by the Director of the British Museum, Neil MacGregor.

The book is described by the publisher as follows: 'Neil MacGregor's *A History of the World in 100 Objects* takes a bold, original approach to human history, exploring past civilizations through the objects that defined them. Encompassing a grand sweep of human history, *A History of the World in 100 Objects* begins with one of the earliest surviving objects made by human hands, a chopping tool from the Olduvai Gorge in Africa, and ends with objects which characterise the world we live in today.'

Adults can listen to the free podcasts and learn more by starting at the following links:

**www.bbc.co.uk/ahistoryoftheworld**

**www.britishmuseum.org/ahistoryoftheworld**

# Jack Trelawny School Author Visits: Assemblies, Skype, and Workshops

Jack makes FREE visits to schools with his 'Edutainment' Shows, which combine 'education with entertainment' and 'learning with fun'.

At the time of writing, December 2013, he has visited more than 1,100 schools and presented his books and story-making ideas to over 250,000 children in the UK.

**Left:**
Presenting the 'Edutainment' Show

**Below:**
Book-signing event after the show

Jack also conducts UK and international Skype visits for schools, during which he talks about stories and writing to children around the world via the internet.

For class workshops, Jack visits schools with his *Story House*, a simple, step-by-step, creative writing system that helps children build their own stories using the expandable Story House template and links from across the curriculum; as well as the widest possible range of other resources, such as the BBC and British Museum.

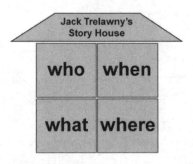

The 'house' starts simply for younger children. It then builds into a complete system which older children can use to create their own new stories and to break down existing stories into understandable parts.

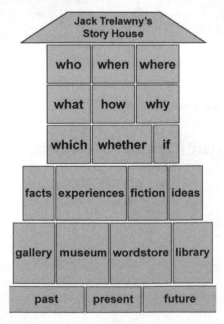

# Arranging and Booking School Author Visits

Teachers can find out more about Jack Trelawny's FREE School Author Visits and fee-based Story House Creative Writing Workshops on the 'Schools' page of his website:

## www.jacktrelawny.com/schools

For more information
or to book a school visit, contact:
Jane Bennett, Events Manager,
Campion Books (Publishers):

**info@campionpublishing.com**